THE SUMMER TRIANGLE

Laurence Rozelle

Genre: Fiction, Young Adult

Table of Contents

Inspired by true events…

The lakes region, a rural part of Upstate where everyone knows everyone and entire families remain close, can be a wonderful place to raise a child; a picturesque world where large deciduous forests, hundreds of lakes, waterfalls, and rolling hills show off their natural beauty for all to see, a place where April showers bring May flowers as spring awakes with an epiphany of years gone by. It is there, in Cayuga Falls, that the innocence of a young girl matures as she engages the real and ever-changing world discovering that even the most beautiful places on earth are not immune from the worst life has to offer. Life is mystery, often without rhyme or reason, and unlocking its secrets can be challenging. However, some secrets are best kept locked away, never to be revealed.

"Believe me, every man has his secret sorrows,
which the world knows not…"
Henry Wadsworth Longfellow

Chapter 1

The Farm, 1984

At twelve years old, Jessie was the boy Jake always dreamt of having. Someone who shared the same interests as he did and didn't mind listening to his corny old stories or lending him a hand when needed, someone with an overwhelming love for life who was blessed with intelligence, confidence, and thoughtfulness, someone who was filled with the curiosity of youth. He could always count on Jessie being by his side. He never thought twice about her being a girl; she was a tomboy, and honestly, he rather liked it that way. Through thick and thin, they forged a relationship that endured both the best and worst that life has to offer.

The first few years were tough, waking up in the middle of the night, changing diapers, and making it through those potty-training years. But as life has it, those times faded in the rear-view mirror, and before Jake could catch his breath, Jessie was finishing out sixth grade. By this time, they were inseparable. Apart from work and school, it seemed there was never a moment when they were not together. In fact, Jessie spent a good amount of time every day at Jake's work after school let out. They were like two peas in a pod. Heck, they even dressed alike, usually in coveralls or jeans, a plaid flannel shirt, and a badly worn pair of leather boots. Their only difference was Jessie loved to talk and ask questions, while Jake was more reserved. Some who didn't know him well might even say reticent, but that didn't bother Jessie. She loved him all the same, like a daughter would love a father.

They lived not far outside the village of Cayuga Falls in the lakes region on a farm Jake would inherit from his dad, who inherited it from his dad, and so on. Their lineage went back to the mid-1800s, when his great-great-grand father, Emery Peabody, lived in Middlesex, Massachusetts, before marrying his childhood sweetheart and moving to the lakes region where they settled on what is now the Peabody farm. That parcel of land has been in the family for more than a century and was the heart and soul of his entire world, or at least that's what Jake believed. His dad, Roy, always talked about the fertility of the land and the generations of Peabody who poured their sweat into it, putting down roots and baring the fruit of their labor. By today's standards, the farm was relatively small at only seventy-two acres but was located on one of the best parcels of land the county has to offer, overlooking Lake Tiohero. Jake had no intentions of ever parting with it and intended to pass it down to Jessie, just as the previous Peabody men had passed it down to their sons.

Working the farm, however, was a different matter as it took a lot of hands and a lot of man-hours to run one, and that is exactly what Jake was missing. Believe me, Jake was no stranger to hard work. He and his brother John grew up on the farm doing chores from the age of four and driving tractors by eight or nine. By the time they were in their teens, there wasn't one piece of machinery on the farm that wasn't being operated by the two Peabody boys. Roy had done a swell job raising them, instilling a hard work ethic, and training them in every aspect of the farm just as his dad had done for him. Times, however, had changed. John was gone, and Roy Peabody was no longer able to endure the demanding work required to run the farm.

Jake felt a little remorse for not working the farm himself but had no plans of letting the land go to waste. Instead, he leased it to Seth Jacobs, who owned a larger track of land just north of the farm. The agreement gave the Jacobs rights to grow and harvest crops for terms of five years and covered fifty-eight of the seventy-two acres. The Peabodys maintained hunting rights, access to all areas that were not cultivated, and of course, they would continue living in the farmhouse perched high on a knoll, offering an unobstructed view of Lake Tiohero. Most of the remaining acreage was along and north of Snyder Creek, which formed the southern border of the farm and was covered in hickory, maple, oak, and beech, along with a few evergreens. Income from the lease was not a lot, but at least it paid for the taxes on the land with a little left over to deposit in the bank for Jessie's future. In the meantime, to supplement that income, Jake worked in town at the Agway Feed & Seed, where he did just about everything, and seeing it was only him and Bob Fleming, who was the boss, well, that left most of the work for him.

Jake could set his watch for 3:15 sharp every afternoon. That would be the time when the front door at the store slammed as Jessie came busting through after school, and today was exactly the same, like clockwork.

"Uncle Jake, Uncle Jake, where are you?" exclaimed Jessie, sounding a little short of breath, "I'm here!"

"I'm in the back working on Mr. Thompson's John Deere," replied Jake as he lay on his back, fumbling to install a nut on the undercarriage. "Wash your hands and grab an apple out of my lunch bucket, then come out here. You can give me a hand with this mower."

Jessie had already raided Jake's lunch bucket from the refrigerator next to the office, skipped washing her hands like most kids, and was making her way through the warehouse toward the back of the store with an apple in her mouth when she ran into Bob.

"Hey, slow down there, kiddo, this isn't a raceway. Where are you going in such a hurry?" asked Bob.

"I came by to see my Uncle Jake," she replied casually. "You know…"

"Okay, but be careful back there, and don't get hurt. I think he's finishing up on that mower," added Bob as Jessie passed him.

The warehouse and work areas in the back of the store were generally safe and hazard-free. Jake made sure of that, but Bob was always protective of Jessie. She was a regular fixture in the store most days, and like everyone else in town, he had grown quite fond of her. He thought of her as the granddaughter he never had.

As she made her way back to where Jake was working, she asked, "What's going on with Mr. Thompson's garden tractor? Did he run into something again?"

Jake laughed. "Well, you know Mr. Thompson, he's blind in one eye and can't see out the other. That deck on his mower is 40 inches wide, and his gate is 42 inches, but somehow, he cannot seem to drive it though without hitting the deck on the gatepost. This time, he bent the front floating mower bracket. Can you hand me that 5/8-inch socket and ratchet over there? Thanks!"

"Why doesn't he get someone to do the mowing for him?" asked Jessie. "You know, I could mow it for five dollars; it would only take me an hour and a half or so, maybe two at the most. I could even use his mower; it's almost like ours except for the hydrostatic transmission."

"Yeah, I'm certain he could afford that if he wanted, but I think it's rather a point of pride with Mr. Thompson. He's no spring chicken, you know, and it's hard for him to surrender to the inevitable."

Jessie understood and, with a little empathy, said, "You mean he's getting old and doesn't want to admit it, right?"

"You got it," said Jake. "Can you hand me that cotter pin? Thanks. Okay, I think this should take care of it for a while, or at least until he runs into the gate again."

They both started laughing, first Jessie, then Jake, and when they looked at each other, it became more infectious and uncontrollable before Jessie caught her breath and said, "Stop, uncle, you're going to make me pee my pants," to which they both started laughing louder.

After getting up from the floor and regaining his composure, Jake tells Jessie, "Why don't you go ahead and sweep out the warehouse and wipe down Mr. Thompson's John Deere so it looks better than it did when he brought it in? Then, we will stop by the IGA on the way home and pick up some butter, flour, and eggs for your grandma. I think she's going to make some of her delicious pancakes in the morning."

"I hope so," said Jessie with anticipation. "Tomorrow is going to be a great day. It's my last day of school for this year, and then it's summer vacation. Hooray! Oh, I can hardly wait! Mr. Randall, our sixth-grade teacher, says it's going to be a hot, dry summer."

"Is that right? How does he know that?" asked Jake as he wiped the grease from his hands.

"*The Farmer's Almanac…* you know, it's really quite accurate," replied Jessie confidently. "He also says we're going to run out of oil by 2050. Is that even possible, Uncle Jake? Are we going to run out of oil?"

"Well, I don't quite know. I suppose your science teacher knows more about that than I do. "When you finish, grab my lunch bucket and meet me out front. I'll be out there talking with Bob for a few minutes."

It took the better part of ten minutes for Jessie to finish sweeping out the warehouse and wiping down the tractor, giving Bob and Jake a few minutes to reflect.

"That young one of yours is growing up fast there, Jake," Bob said. "She's as sharp as a tack. You need to pay more attention to her and watch those boys; you know it's not going to be long."

"I know," replied Jake. "Can you believe she's going to be thirteen soon? She's definitely keeping me straight. Sometimes, I lay awake at night, wondering where the time has gone. You know, it seems like only yesterday that I held her in my arms for the first time."

"Well," sighed Bob as he reminisced, "you're doing a

really fine job with her, Jake. She's a real cutie pie. I wish I had her energy. If you need anything, let me know."

"Thanks, Bob, that means a lot. How's Richard making out these days? I see him at the diner every Saturday, but he's always so busy working we rarely get a chance to talk."

"I suppose he's doing okay," said Bob in a disappointing tone. "I just wish he'd go back to school and really do something with his life. He still feels guilty for not being over there with his buddies… Sorry, Jake, I shouldn't have said… well, enough on that, I'll see you tomorrow; you both have a good night."

After a quick stop at the grocery store and a brief conversation with Linda, the cashier at the IGA, Jake and Jessie jumped into the truck and headed for home; in the summertime, the drive took no more than fifteen-minute, seven miles north on Route 96, take a right on Old Hills Road and the farm was down on the right about three miles. They passed several other small farms and a tiny convenience store with two gas pumps at the intersection on their way home as they talked about school, graduating sixth grade, and moving on to middle school the next year. Jessie's mind was not focused on next year or middle school but rather on summer vacation and all the things she could do – hiking, biking, swimming, and playing outside. She had been counting down the days for the past month, and now it was finally here. Well, almost, just one more day until graduation.

As they pulled off the blacktop and headed down the lane to the farmhouse that was set back 500 feet off the road, they could see Shad running from the back of the house to greet them. He was nine years old but going on sixty-something in dog years, a Golden Retriever, man's best friend. As the pickup came to a stop, Jessie swung open the door and ran toward the house, Shad following closely behind on her heels. Jake just shook his head, stared off toward the east, and took a deep breath of fresh air. From there, he could see just about everything: the farmhouse, garage, barn, and most of the lower farm, which was covered in corn, with a stunning view of Lake Tiohero in the background. He stood there for a few minutes taking it all in, a moment of reflection, before gathering himself and the grocery bags and making his way into the house.

Chapter 2

Last Day of School

Mornings come early at the Peabody's house. Although there are no roosters on the farm to signal the start of the day, both Jake and his mother, Betty, wake up early every morning at 4 a.m., just like clockwork. This, of course, came easily to them after a lifetime of living and working on the farm. Jessie was also an early riser, but not to the same extent. Her day typically started when Shad moseyed into her room, placing his soft, furry muzzle and moist nose against her cheek, giving her a nudge and telling her it was time to get out of bed and that's a bit closer to six, though most of the time, she was already awake lying in bed reading.

That particular morning, however, was special. Being the last day of the school year, Jessie was already up, dressed and making her bed when Shad came into the room. The smell of grandma's delicious pancakes might have also had something to do with her waking up early. According to Jessie, "If you've ever tasted grandma's pancakes, you would never want for anything else to start your morning." They were made with wholesome buttermilk and the loving touch only a grandma has, making them the best ever.

Betty, who was still flipping pancakes in the kitchen, shouted out to Jessie, "Hey Pumpkin, are you up? Your pancakes are ready; wash your hands and come downstairs

– get them while they're still hot."

"Coming, Grandma," she answered excitedly while running down the stairs. "Good morning, Grandpa. Where's Uncle Jake? He didn't leave already, did he? I need a ride to school… he knows I don't like riding the bus."

"Calm down, child," answered Betty. "You know Jake isn't going to leave without you; besides, who is he going to talk to on the way into town? Now eat up before your breakfast gets cold."

About that time, Jake came storming in the back door upset and muttering, "Damn raccoons got into the shed last night, made a real mess. Where the hell was Shad? I didn't hear him bark or anything. Hell of a watch dog, he is."

"Son, Shad is getting older," replied Betty emphatically. "Don't take it out on him. Those raccoons are just a curious, mischievous part of nature and our farm. Now sit down and eat your breakfast; it's going to be a big day."

Jake shook his head and let out a sigh as he thought, *Yeah, but they also carry rabies.*

Jessie smiled, "Pancakes are great, Uncle Jake." She slid the maple syrup across the table before reminding him about her graduation in the afternoon. You need to be there by one o'clock. Mr. Randall says it starts promptly at one, and you need to come home and pick up grandma. You better leave work about 20 minutes after–"

"What would you do without her, Jake?" chimed in a smiling Betty.

"I would probably have less gray hair, that's for sure," chuckled Jake as he gave Jessie a wink. "Come on, let's go;

you don't want me to be late for work and get fired."

Jessie grabbed both her and Jake's lunches off the counter and scurried out the back door toward the pickup. After jumping in and setting the lunches on the seat between her and Jake, she gasped. "Wait, I forgot my graduation cap."

As she flung open her door to go back inside, Jake calmly looked at her and with a cool, even voice, said, "You mean this one."

"Thanks, Uncle Jake; I guess I'm a little excited today," replied Jessie with a sheepish laugh. "I'd probably forget my head if it wasn't attached."

The ride to school was the same as always: down the lane, left on Old Hills Road until you hit Route 96, take a left, go seven miles into town, and the school was on the right about three blocks this side of Agway. Jake was still a little hot around the collar as they began their trip into town. The conversation revolved around the escapades of two raccoons that visited the night before and made a real mess in the shed. By the time they reached Route 96, however, Jake had cooled down, and the talk turned to this afternoon's graduation before ending with a reminder. "Don't forget to pick up grandma."

As Jake drove past the two-story brick school building, he and Jessie could see the staff busy at work setting up the white folding chairs on the freshly manicured lawn. "Wow, check it out," said Jake as he pointed toward the school. "That looks really nice."

"Yeah, it's going to be great! I hope Grandma brings her camera. Can you remind her?"

"Sure, we'll take lots of pictures."

The school bell signaling the start of class didn't ring until 7:45, and Jake had to be at work by 7:30 to open the store, so in typical fashion, Jessie started her day in town just as she would finish it, at work with her Uncle Jake.

From there, the walk to school was straight down Main Street past the U.S. Postal Office, First National Bank of Cayuga Falls, and Volunteer Firehouse, all of which were on the east side of the street. The school was situated on the opposite side of Main, across from the white Methodist church.

The morning could not have been more beautiful, about 65 degrees with a clear, blue sky. "Simply a lovely day for a graduation," she thought. The air was filled with the sweet smell of fresh-cut grass, meaning summer had finally arrived. As Jessie strolled up the sidewalk leading to the front doors of the school, she was greeted by many of the faculty working outside that morning. She knew nearly everyone, having either been in their class or met them at assembly. Mr. Randall was also out-front speaking with Mr. Atkinson, the elementary school principal who was orchestrating the setup for graduation.

"Good morning, Miss Peabody," said Mr. Randall in a friendly and cheerful manner. "Do you have time to help us setup?"

Jessie looked at Mr. Randall, and then glanced cautiously at Mr. Atkinson hesitating slightly before replying, "No, I have got to go inside, thank you."

Normally, Jessie would love to help Mr. Randall, who she respected immensely, but today, she thought it best to skip that opportunity. She was always leery of Mr. Atkinson ever since fourth grade when she was sent to his office with Beth Stewart for causing a ruckus in class. This was the one and only blemish on Jessie's elementary school record and, frankly, one that she wasn't very proud of.

Beth had just returned from being out sick the prior two days and asked Jessie what homework assignments she had missed. Jessie sat right behind her in Miss Carter's class, and for whatever reason, Jessie gave Beth the wrong assignments. When Beth found out that Jessie had lied to her, the two of them got into a loud argument, and a few papers went flying through the air. Miss Carter would have none of that nonsense in her classroom and sent both girls off to the principal's office. Their punishment that day was to stand straight and tall in front of Mr. Atkinson's desk holding a stack of books out in front of themselves for five minutes, which seemed like an eternity. From that time on, she always thought Mr. Atkinson was a mean old man. She and Beth, well, they have never spoken another word to each other since that day in fourth grade.

Leaving work early to attend Jessie's graduation that afternoon would not be a problem for Jake. He had already spoken with Bob a few weeks earlier about taking the time off, and of course, Bob said yes. His exact words were, "Jake, there's no other place you should be. I might even put a closed sign in the window and go there myself."

Jake did not wait until twenty minutes past twelve to leave work, as Jessie suggested; he left precisely at noon. He wanted to give himself enough time to change out of his coveralls and into something a little more appropriate for a graduation. The thought of ditching the work boots and denim for some dress shoes and slacks, which he hadn't worn in years, pressed against his nature, but he would do it for Jessie. This was her day.

Betty was ready to go when Jake pulled up to the farmhouse. She wore a soft, pastel dress fit for summertime in the lakes region. Since the forecast called for sunny skies, clear and about 78 degrees at the start of the ceremony, she decided to wear her stylish large brim hat with flowers to keep the sun off her neck and face. Betty didn't have many occasions to dress up, so she relished the opportunity to do so for Jessie's graduation. Slipping into the dress and seeing her reflection in the mirror brought back memories of years past. "Oh my gosh, where have the years gone?" she thought.

Roy chose not to attend Jessie's graduation ceremony at the school. He seldom left the farmhouse after suffering his heart attack and stroke thirteen years earlier. The only times he did leave the farm were for his doctor's appointments and the family reunion. After two years of rehabilitation following his stroke, Roy could get around the house with his walker, but the stroke left the right side of his face paralyzed, and his speech slurred and often garbled. He would, however, be fine staying at home on his own for a couple of hours.

Back at school, the faculty and staff were busy lining the sixth graders up, beginning in the vestibule and going down the main hallway in preparation for the ceremony. Although there were two six-grade classes, Mr. Randall and Mrs. Beverley's, the students lined up alphabetically as one group and then marched out to take their seats. The ceremony began after all the parents and guests were seated. Before Mr. Atkinson gave his speech and handed out diplomas, the crowd was treated to a not-so-tight rendition of the Star-Spangled Banner, courtesy of the CF High School prep band, and an invocation delivered by Pastor Paul from the Methodist Church located across the street.

Jessie was lined up behind Lori Palmer and in front of Ronnie Richards, both of whom she had gone to school with since kindergarten. The hallway was filled with excitement, nervous laughter, and the chattering of fifty-seven soon-to-be junior high school students.

"Can you believe it, Jessie? This is really happening," Lori said. "We are going to graduate. My mom says your uncle should get married; it's strange for a man in his thirties to not have a wife. She also said that your uncle dated your mom before she married your dad, and that is why he never got married."

Jessie tried not to think about it and shrugged off the implications, instead replying, "I can't wait for seventh grade." Still, Lori's words hurt deeply, as Jessie often felt different from the others for not having her own set of parents.

Ronnie, hoping to impress the girls, chimed in, saying, "I'm going to be the star of the junior high basketball team."

Both girls laughed and giggled the way young girls do, all the while thinking, *Sure you are.*

This infuriated Ronnie, who turned red in the face before turning away from the girls pretending that conversation never happened.

At one o'clock sharp, everyone stood as the colors were posted, and the band began playing the national anthem, signaling the start of the ceremony.

Another half-hour passed before Mr. Atkinson called Jessie's name. She was number forty-three on the list of six-graders to receive their diplomas. Her heart started racing when she heard Lori Palmer's name called, and she thought she might faint when she heard her own. Hopefully, Mr. Atkinson would not recall that terrible day when she visited his office and stood there in front of his desk, that terrible day that she and Beth Stewart had a falling out. "How will I be able to look him in the eyes?" she thought. She prayed for a quick shake-and-take without any words spoken. That, however, would not be the case. When her name was called, she nervously walked across the stage, dreading the encounter. To her astonishment, when Mr. Atkinson placed the diploma in her hand, he bent over slightly and with warm eyes and a soft voice, whispered, "Well done, Ms. Jessica Peabody, it's been a real pleasure having you here. Best wishes to you going forward."

Those warm words brought tears to her eyes. Jessie could hardly believe her ears. For two years, she felt shame for the incident between her and Beth in fourth grade, and now Mr. Atkinson, who she thought was a mean old principal, congratulated her with kind words. Whether it was the excitement of graduation, the anxiety of facing him, or the relief that it was now over, Jessie could not hold back the tears.

After all the diplomas were handed out and the pastor

gave benediction, the graduates all turned around facing their parents, guests, and loved ones, and on the count of three, all tossed their graduation caps into the air as high as they possibly could. The air filled with laughter, applause, and many congratulations while the band played the high school fight song, and that concluded the elementary school graduation ceremony.

School was now officially over for the year, but the celebration continued long after they returned home. Betty had put a roast in the crockpot for dinner and made a fresh cherry pie that morning. Jake had picked some flowers from the garden and put them in a vase on the table. Today was an incredibly special day for Jessie. It was more than just the last day of the school year; it was the end of elementary school, a time for leaving her childhood behind and entering her adolescent and teenage years, a time for her to be taken more seriously in the future.

Betty was keen to spot the changes that were taking place. She knew they were coming and saw them before Jessie or Jake even became aware of them. Summer would be a special time, and she was looking forward to being there for Jessie. Jake, on the other hand, would probably be the last to know. The next few months were sure to see many changes, and Betty could only hope that everyone was ready.

Chapter 3

Saturday Ritual

Saturday was the best day of the week in Jessie's eyes. She saw it not only as a non-school day but also as a day to spend with her uncle surveying the farm, fixing that which needed repairing and playing with Shad, but her favorite part of Saturdays was going to the diner to start the day, just her and her Uncle Jake. For them, the trip had become a ritual over the past five years or so, like going to church, a place to gather, seeing faces one hasn't seen in a while, and listening to all sorts of stories. School was okay for socializing, but going to the diner with her Uncle Jake and experiencing everyone sharing their stories and discussing the news gave her a sense of community.

Every Friday night before bedtime, Jake would always say, "You need to get up early if you want to go to the diner with me in the morning. We need to get an early start so we can get a good seat."

"I know," she always replied in a polite tone. Waking early, however, was never a problem for her. If Shad failed to wake her, which he never did, Uncle Jake and Grandma would always make plenty of noise as they rustled around the kitchen early in the morning making their coffee and talking. Just because it was Saturday didn't mean the Peabody's didn't rise and shine before the sun did; it was bred in them.

Jessie was not the only one who liked going to the diner on Saturday mornings, spending the entire day together and doing the things they did. Jake received just as much pleasure out of the day as Jessie, maybe even more. He might not admit it outright, but Jake always enjoyed showing off his niece to everyone in town, just as any proud father would. She was the "twinkle in his eyes."

This was the first Saturday after school let out for vacation, and although not even seven in the morning, the diner was already filling up. As luck had it, there were still two seats next to each other at the counter; otherwise, they would have to settle for a booth. In Jessie's mind, sitting at the counter was a hundred times better than being relegated to a booth. The counter was where all the action and excitement was, and from there, she could not only see everything and everyone but could also hear most of the conversations if she listened carefully. The diner could be loud with all kinds of commotion – coffee cups clanking, silverware scraping plates, chairs shuffling, and, of course, everyone talking. Sitting at the counter also offered an unobstructed view into the kitchen, where she could watch Emily hand Richard the tickets as she yelled out the orders. Jessie thought working in such a place where the rich aroma of coffee mixed with the wholesome smell of bacon and eggs sizzling on the grill had to be fun.

Richard was Bob Fleming's only son and two years older than John. Upon graduating high school, he left Cayuga Falls and went on to college for two years before dropping out and coming home. Scuttlebutt had it that Mr. Fleming had sent him off to college to avoid the draft and the war in Southeast Asia. He was one of the lucky ones; as they said, "If you had the dough, you didn't have to go." Many, however, didn't have the means or inclination for college and were stuck working on the farms with their families, hoping their draft numbers would not be drawn.

Emily was Jake's age, single, and quite a sight with her long auburn hair, cute dimples, and freckles on her nose. Jake knew her well. They spent many of their younger years sharing the same classrooms, eating lunch in the school cafeteria, and riding the bus together every morning. She was the youngest in the Jacobs household and Seth's only daughter.

As busy as the diner was, no more than a minute passed before Emily poured Jake a cup of coffee and placed a small orange juice in front of Jessie. She then leaned slightly forward resting both of her elbows on the counter, looked Jake squarely in the eyes, and asked, "Who's that cutie you're with this morning, Jake? You know, I might get jealous."

She smiled, gave Jessie a wink, and said, "I'll be back in a moment to take your orders."

"What would you like this morning?" asked Jake. "Do you see anything on the menu that looks good?"

"I want the eggs, bacon, and hash browns," Jessie hungrily replied as she felt the emptiness in the pit of her stomach.

"Yeah, that sounds like a winner to me also; I guess we should get two of those this morning."

"I think she likes you, Uncle Jake," teased Jessie.

"Who?" replied Jake, pretending he didn't know whom

she was talking about.

"Emily. I think Emily likes you."

"Oh… well, that's nonsense; why would you think that?"

"Well, she was flirting with you for one thing, and I don't know, but she has that look in her eyes."

Jake was about to explain his friendship with Emily when she returned to take their order. "Have you decided yet?" she asked.

"I think we'll both have the eggs and bacon with hash browns. I'd also like a little more coffee if you could…"

"And how do you want your eggs this morning Jakey, over easy like usual?"

"That would be nice," stammered Jake as he slowly looked over at Jessie.

"How about you, sweetie? Did you want anything else?"

"No, I'm fine, thank you," smiled Jessie as she giggled. "You see…"

Jessie watched as Emily turned around, handed the ticket to Richard, and yelled out their order. The diner was as busy as she could recall ever seeing it. Emily was methodically making her way from customer to customer, topping off their coffee cups and taking orders while Richard slaved over the hot grill, tending to the bacon, eggs, and sausage.

The diner was especially noisy this particular morning as it filled to capacity. There were three men sitting at the end of the counter discussing the Memorial Day parade that took place two weeks earlier. All three were veterans of foreign wars who were lamenting over how small the parade was this year, especially compared to the parade of '76, which, of course, drew a much larger crowd, being it was a bicentennial year. Then, there was a family of four sitting in a booth near the front door. Jessie wasn't sure of their names, but she had seen the man in the Agway Feed & Seed a few times while visiting her Uncle Jake. Their two children were small – Jessie thought them to be around five or six – and they were definitely acting out their ages, in and out of the booth, dropping their utensils, and in general, just being loud. Mr. Randall and his wife were in a booth at the other end of the diner, both were busy eating with little discernible conversation. On the other side of Jake sat Linda from the IGA and one of her friends. They were discussing the carnival scheduled to visit Cayuga Falls two weekends after the Fourth of July. Jake was telling Linda that Friday nights were usually the best time for the carnival. The rest of the diner was filled with local farmers, Mr. Jacobs being one of them, and that made Jessie wonder, "Does Emily do all the cooking at home?"

Breakfast at the diner was amazing, as usual. Jessie sat there taking everything in and letting her food settle while waiting for Jake to finish his second cup of coffee. After twenty minutes or so, he asked Jessie, "Are we ready to go?" He then turned toward Emily. "I think we are ready; what's the damage?"

Emily smiled, "I'll bring it right over, sweetie; give me a minute."

When she returned, Jake noticed that she had left him a note written in red ink on the receipt paper along with a big smiley face. It said, "Are you taking me to the carnival this year?"

Jake smiled to himself and thought, *Yeah, that would be nice, just like old times. I haven't been on a date in a long time.*

Jessie also saw the note but said nothing. She wasn't sure what to think about it, or for that matter, how she should feel about it. She assumed that Uncle Jake and her were going to the carnival together like every other year.

The drive back to the farm seemed longer than usual. Jessie was thinking about the note Emily wrote and whether she should ask her uncle outright who he was planning on taking to the carnival. She liked Emily a lot, but this was the carnival. *He always takes me to the carnival. Maybe he will tell her no, but what if he doesn't? What then?* Jessie wrestled with these thoughts and feelings, but that wasn't the only thing on her mind. She just wanted to get home, go to her room, and be comforted by Shad, her loyal companion.

Jake didn't pay much attention to Jessie on the way home. Emily was still in his thoughts, and the more he thought about her, the more he felt a warmth brewing inside. This wouldn't be the first time they went to the carnival together or on a date, for that matter. He recalled his high school years when he and Emily enjoyed going to the carnival with John and Mary, before they were married, but that was long ago before they both passed away and Jessie became part of his life. The possibility of a renewed relationship with Emily intrigued him.

As Jake pulled off the road and headed down the lane toward the farmhouse, Jessie asked, "Can you stop? I want to walk from here.”

“Sure,” said Jake, a bit confused, “If that’s what you want… Can you also check the mail and bring it up to the house?”

Jessie left the vehicle and Jake continued down the lane, parking the truck next to the garage, which was situated between the house and barn. As he ambled toward the house, he watched Jessie walking slowly up the lane, with her head down, carrying the mail in her right hand. Before he reached the back door, Shad came scurrying around the corner, wagging his tail, passing him by, and running down the lane to greet Jessie, who welcomed him with open arms.

Betty met Jake at the back door, “Mr. Ramsey dropped by this morning with a delivery. I had him put it in the garage as you asked.”

“Excellent! Thanks, Mom, I appreciate that.”

“Where’s Jessie?”

“She’s coming,” answered Jake in a slightly subdued voice. “I think something’s bugging her, though. She seemed a little quiet coming home, and that girl is never lost for words.”

“Did something happen this morning between the two of you?” asked Betty inquisitively.

“No, not that I remember. As usual, we had a rather enjoyable time at the diner. I’ll tell you what; even Emily was particularly friendly this morning, asking if I would take her to the carnival this year.” Then, with a poorly stifled grin and a sly raise of his eyebrows, he said, “And I’ve got to say, I’m looking forward to doing just that.”

Betty paused at this and turned slowly, “Does Jessie

know that?"

"I'm not sure, I suppose it's possible. Emily wrote it on my receipt; why?" asked Jake, looking a little puzzled.

"Son, did you even consider what Jessie might be thinking? You told her you were taking her to the carnival just as you do every year, the two of you together. She probably feels hurt, confused, and left out. Did you even consider that, Jake? For heaven's sake, she's only twelve."

Jake was mystified and a little upset with the tone in his mother's voice, but deep down, he knew that she was right; sometimes, he could be inconsiderate. He was about to reply when Jessie came walking through the back door.

"How are you, Pumpkin?" asked Betty curiously.

"Fine," said Jessie. "I'm going up to my room with Shad." There, she laid on her bed staring up at the ceiling, thinking about her Uncle Jake, Emily and the carnival, and what Lori Palmer said prior to graduation. *Why would she say that? Was there something going on between my uncle and my mother? I need to find out.*

Back in the kitchen, Betty looked at Jake, shook her head, and went back to her chores. "We will talk about this later."

Chapter 4

New Kids in Town

The following morning, Jessie woke at the usual time and ran downstairs to the kitchen. Betty was already sitting at the table with a cup of coffee, and Shad was whining at the back door. Jake was out in the garage, puttering around and making himself busy.

"The sun's been up for thirty minutes, Pumpkin; you better take him out for a run. Check and see what Jake's up to in the garage; he may need your help. I'll give you both a yell when breakfast is ready."

"Okay, Grandma," she said, and off they went, running out the back, screen door slamming.

Shad, which was short for Shadrack, still had some juice left in his legs, even at his age. The two of them ran down the lane to the road and back to the front yard as fast as they possibly could. It was a race that neither wanted to lose, and they both knew it. Jessie gave it her all, but her fresh legs were no match for Shad's four. When they reached the grass, Jessie fell to the ground and rested on her back, catching her breath, with Shad licking her face.

The garage was still somewhat dark inside, even though the sun was up. The big sliding doors to the east were open but the florescent lights over the workbench were not on. The garage itself was large enough for three vehicles and a workspace, but today, it was half empty, as Jake always parked his truck outside during the summer months. He did, however, keep the only tractor still left on the farm parked inside, along with his snowmobile, which Jessie enjoyed riding in the wintertime with him. As she made her way around the tractor, Jessie could hear Jake fiddling with something in the corner, but she couldn't tell what exactly.

"Guess what, Uncle Jake, I just saw some cars in the driveway next door at the Jenkins place," said Jessie as she entered the garage.

"Oh, is that right?" replied Jake. "I don't think there's been anyone in that house for two years now. Maybe we're going to have some new neighbors."

When Jake came into sight, Jessie's eyes got as big as saucers. From there, she could see him crouched down alongside a motorcycle. Well, it wasn't exactly a motorcycle in terms of size, more like a baby motorcycle, but Jessie knew exactly what it was: a Yamaha 80 minibike. Jessie was speechless with a grin from ear to ear.

"What do you think?' said Jake. "It's used but in really good condition."

"Is it for me, Uncle Jake? You got this for me?"

"Yeah, I did," said Jake, feeling quite satisfied. "Mr. Ramsey came in the store on Monday asking Bob if he could hang a for sale notice up, said his boy outgrew it. Anyway, I told him I would take it. I see how you look at the other boys riding their bikes. This will be a good bike for you to ride around the farm. I don't want to see or hear about you racing it, though; just be safe and always wear your helmet, just as we do when riding the snowmobile."

"I know, I know," she repeated excitedly as she gave her

Uncle Jake a wonderful, loving embrace. "When did you get it?"

"Mr. Ramsey dropped it off yesterday morning while we were at the diner. I wanted to surprise you. Let's go in now and have some breakfast. We'll have plenty of time to check it out after that. I'm sure your grandma has something good for us this morning."

Jessie was on cloud nine; she couldn't believe Uncle Jake actually bought her a minibike. She thought, *How many times did I tell him I wanted to have one, how many times did I point out the other kids riding them on their farms, how many times I thought, and now. Finally, I have my own. This summer is going to be the best!*

After breakfast, Jake and Jessie went back to the garage to check out the bike. Jessie already had a bicycle and knew how to ride it well, so balance would not be a problem. Jake showed her where the brakes, accelerator, clutch, and shifting levers were and how they operated. For the most part, it did not operate much differently than the snowmobile, which Jake had let her drive on occasions with him right behind her on the back. The shifting lever, however, was down near the left foot peg, and the rear brake pedal was down near the right foot peg. Most everything else was the same or very similar.

After some instructions and a brief demonstration by Jake, the time had come for Jessie to give it a go. After a quick tug on her helmet strap and making sure the bike was in neutral, she balanced the bike with her left leg and gave a big push down on the kick-starter with her right leg. The bike started at once.

"Okay, remember, one down and three up," said Jake, referring to the shifting pattern of the four-speed transmission. "Ease the clutch out slowly and give it just a little gas so as not to stall the engine."

"It wasn't terribly difficult," she thought. She had driven their snowmobile before, and the garden tractor, which she drives every week to mow the grass, has five speeds. Off she went, down the lane to the edge of the road and back, moving up and down through the gears. She could feel the rush of adrenalin and wind in her face as she accelerated, giving her a sense of freedom and power. Operating the bike wasn't difficult at all; she was a natural.

After the first trip down and back, she stopped beside Jake and asked, "How was that? Did I do okay?"

"You did perfect, kiddo," he said with a big smile on his face. "Listen, just ride on the lane between the barn and the road for now. I'm going inside for a bit."

Jessie continued having fun riding back and forth between the barn and the road. At one point, she stopped near the road and took a moment to scope out the Jenkins place, which was nearly 300 yards south of their farm on the same side of the road. Indeed, it looked as though they had new neighbors. From the end of the lane, she saw what appeared to be a man and two boys unloading a pickup truck filled with all sorts of items. *Uncle Jake was right*, she thought. *I wonder how old these boys are.* Jessie rode her new bike back to the house, parked it in the garage, and ran inside. She could hardly wait to tell everyone the news.

"Guess what, Uncle Jake, you were right. We have new neighbors. I saw them; they were unloading their truck, and they had two boys."

"Okay, well, let's not be bothering them today. I'm sure they have a lot of work to do moving in," said Jake. "I'm taking your grandma to church in a few minutes or whenever she's ready. We'll be leaving soon, and I don't want you riding that new bike when no one is here, got it?"

"Yes sir," replied Jessie like a good little soldier.

Jake and Betty left the house a few minutes later. Church service started at ten sharp every Sunday morning, and Betty rarely missed going. The services lasted an hour or so, depending on how long Pastor Paul spoke, but Jake never went inside. Churches had a way of making him feel uncomfortable.

While Jake and Betty were gone, Jessie decided she and Shad should take a walk around the farm. They headed off down the lane and took a left at the road, strolling between the rows of corn planted by Mr. Jacobs and the asphalt. Soon, they were at the edge of the farm, which was separated from the Jenkins place by Snyder Creek. Arriving at this point on the farm was not by accident. From there, it was only a couple hundred feet to the neighbor's house, and Jessie could see everything clearly. The truck was unloaded, and the boys were running around the house, playing and yelling at each other.

Shad became excited and started barking, wagging his tail, and jumping around when he saw the boys, and that, in turn, got their attention. Jessie heard the taller boy say, "Come on, let's go and say hello," as they both ran toward the creek. Shad couldn't wait; he splashed across the creek and met the boys on the opposite side. The creek was not very wide or deep at this point, but it had plenty of options for crossing: rocks, stepping stones, logs, and the like.

Jessie exclaimed, "Don't worry, he won't bite you. He loves everyone. His name is Shad."

The boys were not intimidated at all. Before Jessie could even spit out all her words, the two boys and Shad were all rolling around on the ground, laughing, playing, and getting to know each other. "What's your name?" asked the oldest.

"Jessie, Jessie Peabody, what's yours?"

"Jimmy, and that's Brian, but we call him Oscar because he's such an actor. We just moved in today."

"Yeah, I know; I saw you unloading the truck earlier. What's your last name?"

"Jenkins. This was our grandfather's house, but he passed away several years ago. Dad wanted to move back and said it was a beautiful place to grow up. Outside of it being greener than the city, it doesn't look like there's a lot to do here. I didn't see any movie theaters or skating rinks. Do you have a mall?"

Jessie laughed, "Of course, we have a mall, silly; it's over in Millsburg. I think they might also have a skating rink… I know they have a movie theater; I've been there. What grade are you going into this year?"

"I'm going into seventh, and Oscar's going into fifth grade this year," replied Jimmy. "How about you?"

"Seventh also, maybe we'll have the same classes this year. Anyway, I've got to go before my uncle gets home. He took my grandma to church this morning, the same as he does every Sunday. Maybe I will see you later. Come on, Shad, let's go, boy. Nice meeting you."

Shad came bounding across the creek, and the two began their trek back to the farmhouse. They took their time meandering east along the tree line until they reached the end of the cornfield. Jessie enjoyed hiking this route as she could hear the leaves on the trees dancing in the breeze and the rippling sounds of Snyder Creek in the background; sounds that were music to her ears. At the end of the field, the two of them took a left, heading north, making their way straight across the farm, along the hedgerow, before arriving at the back of the house near the shed.

On their walk back home, Jessie noticed that the corn in the field was knee high. She remembered how Uncle Jake always said, "Corn should be knee high by the Fourth of July," and that would be a good indicator for the year's harvest. At first, she was delighted but then realized that her knees were much lower than Uncle Jake's, and that brought her some concern, as the fourth was only a week away. "Are we having a bad year this year?" she wondered. "It has been very dry and a little warmer than usual."

Jessie's thoughts returned to the two boys, Jimmy and Oscar, who she just met this morning and who were moving in right next door to her. She wondered what they liked to do for fun and what the city was like. With all this great outdoors, why did Jimmy say it didn't look like there was anything to do? She could think of a hundred things to do. She needed to show them just how great living here in the lakes region was with all its beauty and natural wonders.

Jake and Betty returned from church moments later. Betty was still talking about Pastor Paul's sermon as she came through the back door, and Jake was pretending to listen politely, although he didn't hear a word she said. They all sat down for a nice Sunday lunch and talked about the weather, this year's corn prediction, Jessie's new bike, and, of course, the new kids in town. Jessie would then spend the rest of the afternoon riding her new bike back and forth down the lane between Old Hills Road and the far eastern reaches of the farm above Lake Tiohero.

Chapter 5

Family Reunion

Because this year's Fourth of July fell in the middle of the week on a Wednesday, the Peabody annual family reunion was planned for the following Saturday. Like every other year, this reunion will be held at the Glen Point State Park on the east side of the lake. Although the park was only ten miles away from the farm as the crow flies, it took nearly an hour to drive around the southern end of the lake through Millsburg and up the east side before reaching it. The 750-acre park was created in 1925 and offered miles of natural trails, camping, picnicking, and a marina with a small bait and tackle shop where one can also rent canoes.

Jessie always loved going to the park and watching the people enjoy everything summer had to offer, and since they went there on or about every Fourth of July, it was always busy and very festive, with everyone celebrating the holiday. The park was full of music, people laughing and playing games, along with the smell of franks, burgers, and chicken on the grill. Frisbees flew through the air everywhere, with dogs running and jumping, trying to catch them as their owners shouted words of encouragement. In Jessie's eyes, there was never a dull moment. Saturday in the park was a real treat, and she looked forward to this year's reunion.

Betty spent the Friday before the reunion working

tirelessly in the kitchen preparing a few pies for the gathering, and Jessie stayed by her side doing whatever she could to help. Betty was the kitchen commander, barking out orders, and Jessie was the loyal soldier, obeying every command. Betty thought, a *disciplined and organized process leads to success*; at least, this is what her mother taught her.

Her directions were precise. "Okay, Pumpkin, get the big glass bowl out and put it at this end of the table with the flour, shortening, salt, and a little water. At the other end of the table, take seven Granny Smith apples, peel, and core, and then slice them up like I showed you."

"Do you want me to make the dough after I finish the apples, Grandma?"

"No, that's okay, Pumpkin, I'll make the dough. You can add cinnamon, regular sugar, and brown sugar to the apples and then mix them together. Don't forget the teaspoon of vanilla and a tablespoon of lemon juice."

"Okay… I was wondering, Grandma, why hasn't Uncle Jake ever married?"

"I can't rightly say, Pumpkin. I guess he hasn't found the right person yet. Why?"

"Is it true that Uncle Jake dated my mom before she married Dad?"

That question caught Betty off guard. "For heaven's sake, where did you hear that?"

"Lori Palmer's mother told her, and she told me about it at graduation."

"Well, all of those kids hung around together when they were teenagers. I don't think it was anything more serious than holding hands and going to a movie.

Grandma's answer seemed to make sense, she thought, *but if so, why would Lori add, that's why your uncle never got married? There must be more that she doesn't know or doesn't want to say.*

The baking process continued until the pair had successfully prepared both an apple and cherry pie from scratch and slid them into the oven. They spent the next forty-five minutes wisely cleaning the kitchen and packing the tote with paper plates, napkins, cups, and utensils needed for the next day's outing. By the time they finished, the pies were golden brown and ready to take out of the oven.

"Who's going to be at the park tomorrow, Grandma?"

"I'm not sure exactly who will show up, Pumpkin. Roy's sister Marge will probably come with her daughter Harriet, who is your aunt on Roy's side of the family, and of course, she will bring her two boys, who are a few years older than you. My brother Allan said he was coming, but he wasn't sure if his wife Joan would make it; she hadn't been feeling well. Both of their children, your Uncle Rich and Aunt Pat, usually make it, so your cousins Diane, Linda, and Steven should be there as well. You never know who's going to show up at these reunions until they happen."

"Can I go outside now, Grandma?" asked Jessie hopefully. "I want to ride my bike for a while and go see if Jimmy and Oscar can play."

"Okay, but stay on the farm, please. And make sure you wear your helmet!" reminded Betty as the back door slammed shut.

Jessie ran out of the house lickety-split before Grandma came up with something else for her to do. She raced to the garage and pushed open the sliding doors just enough to get her bike through. First, though, she needed to put gas in the tank because it was still on reserve from her last ride. Uncle Jake normally kept a red, five-gallon metal gas can in the garage, which was at least half full of petrol for the mower. After a quick service, she tightened down the gas cap and was on her way.

She would make a big loop down the lane, along the road, back along the tree line, beside the hedgerow, and past the shed. The second time around, she would stop next to Snyder Creek across from the Jenkins place and see if the boys were outside, which they were. They heard her go zipping by the first time and came over to see if she would stop and say hello.

After finding neutral on her bike, she shut off the engine, put the kickstand down, and jumped off. Both Jimmy and Oscar were already crossing the creek, going from rock to rock, making sure they didn't get their shoes wet.

"What are you two up to today?" she asked, hoping they could come over to the farm.

"Dad has us cleaning up the yard," said Jimmy, looking dejected. "It's a mess."

Oscar piped up, "Yeah, it's a real mess over here. It hasn't been mowed or leaves raked, or anything since Grandpa lived here."

Jessie asked if they could hang out together in the afternoon. If so, she would ride her bike home and bring Shad back with her.

"Unfortunately, not this afternoon," said Jimmy. "Maybe tomorrow, that's if we can get this job done."

Jessie was disappointed; she was hoping to have someone to engage with this afternoon. "Well, I probably won't see you for a couple of days then," she said sadly. "We have our family reunion tomorrow. We have one every year at this time, and I get to see a lot of people I don't know or haven't seen in the last year." She would spend the rest of her day riding her bike and playing outside with Shad.

Saturday came, and it was now time for the Peabody family to load up and head out. They would take Betty's car since everyone, including Shad, was going. Jake would drive, and Betty would ride shotgun. Jessie and Roy would sit in the back with Shad between them. Everything else, including Roy's walker and a folding chair for him to sit in, along with a blanket to cover his legs, were tucked away in the trunk. They needed to make a quick stop at the IGA and grab a bag of ice before driving to the lake's far side.

Jake pulled into the park precisely at noon and drove counterclockwise around the perimeter road before stopping at the second pavilion. Most of the family was already there, and Allan had the grills fired up. Betty was first to exit the car and lent Roy a hand getting out, helping him balance against the rear door until Jessie arrived by his side with the walker. Betty made her way to the pavilion with both pies in hand while Jessie walked beside Roy to aid him if needed. Jake was left to take care of the chair, blanket, bag of ice, and tote full of the basic necessities for picnicking, all the while muttering, "Really."

Everyone was very pleased to see everyone else, and

there were plenty of smiles and hugs. Betty's brother Allan was the first to speak with Jessie, asking, "What's your name, sweetie?"

To which she replied, "Jessie," in a shy manner.

"Why, that just can't be," he said. "The Jessie I know is only this tall," he said as he put his hand down next to his knee and began laughing. He then gave her a big hug and commented on how tall she was now and how grown up she looked.

Of course, this made her feel incredibly good inside; someone actually took notice that she wasn't a child anymore. She continued mingling with all the relatives, telling them how she was now in Junior High School, seventh grade, and that she had her own Yamaha motorcycle. At that time, Aunt Pat arrived with her cousins Linda and Steven. Shad was already there, next to their car, tail wagging in anticipation and ready to greet them before they even had a chance to open their doors. Linda was Jessie's age, and Steven was four years older, already in high school.

Everyone who was coming was now there; Betty was standing behind Roy with her hands on his shoulders in a comforting fashion as he sat in his chair out of the sun underneath the pavilion. Jake was talking with his cousin Rich about this year's corn crop and the dry summer they were having. Rich asked Jake if he had his eyes on any girls, to which Jake replied, maybe. Marge, Harriet, and Pat were all sitting at the picnic tables, catching up with each other and discussing the events of the previous year. Much of the conversation centered on Jessie, how much she had grown over the past year, and how her life was living with her uncle and grandparents. Pat, who never cares what other people think, asked, "How's Jessie coping without Mary as she gets older; is she missing that mother figure in her life?"

Betty replied briskly, "She's fine; everything is fine." She tried to change the subject, but those questions burned inside her, making her feel uneasy and inadequate.

Marge joined in on the inquisition. "Does she ask a lot of questions about her parents? She's at that age now, it must be difficult."

Betty responded. "No, not at all," even though she knew that wasn't the case, but she hated the insinuations. *Sometimes family can be a real pain in the ass,* she thought.

Jessie and all her cousins were far too busy playing and running around barefoot in the grass with Shad to hear any of the conversations taking place among the adults. They were in their own world, enjoying everything the park had to offer.

"Come get your burgers and hotdogs!" Allan proclaimed as he wiped the sweat from his forehead. "Ketchup, mustard, and buns are right over there on the table next to the paper plates and cups."

Jessie and her cousins were first in line. They were famished after all that playing and running around. Even Shad had a hot dog after Allan accidentally dropped one on the ground for him.

"Where's your manners Shadrack?" asked Jessie.

Shad began barking as if to ask for seconds, to which Allan happily obliged.

After lunch, Jessie asked Uncle Jake if it was okay for

her to walk up the glen to see the waterfalls with her cousins.

Jake replied, "Take Shad with you and stay away from the edge. I doubt there's a lot of water coming over the falls, but the rocks will still be wet, so be careful. Be back here in an hour, okay? Oh, and put your shoes on."

The four of them, Jessie, Linda, Steven, and Shad, took off across the park looking for the trailhead at the start of the glen. The glen was a narrow gorge with two-hundred-foot cliffs carved out of the hillside by water over thousands of years. At the trailhead was a large sign framed in timber, educating visitors about the history of the park and the evolution of the glen. From there, beautiful flagstone walkways and paths with stonewalls with rails were chiseled out of the rock facing alongside the gorge by the Civilian Conservation Corps back in the 1930s. There were two trails leading to the upper glen, one being the Rim Trail and the other the Gorge Trail, which was Jessie's favorite as it wound over, around and behind cascading falls of water. Jessie thought it was the most gorgeous scenery in the entire lakes region, a natural wonder that left her spellbound. The trip to the upper glen was two miles long, but they would turn around at the halfway point after walking behind her favorite waterfalls and taking in the spray and cool mist of water spilling over the rocks from above.

Jessie enjoyed Steven's company as she rarely hung around with anyone his age. They talked mostly about life on the farm and current events happening around the world. She was impressed with his knowledge and views on a wide range of topics, although she sometimes felt a little inadequate in expressing her own thoughts.

After a slow march back to the lower park, it would be time for another plate of food and a piece of Grandma's pie. Jessie thought both pies were great, but Cherry was her favorite. She would savor every bite as she sat there watching her relatives begin packing up as the reunion slowly came to an end.

Jessie asked Jake. "Can we take a canoe out on the lake for a little bit before we leave?"

"Not today," answered Jake kindly. "Dad is pretty tired, and it's been a long day for him, so I think we better get on the road. We'll do it another time."

"Okay then, I guess I'm ready," said Jessie, "Come on Shad, let's go, it's time to go home."

Chapter 6

Questions

Sunday morning came and went with Jessie spending most of her time near Snyder Creek playing with Jimmy and Oscar. Jake spent his time having coffee at the diner while Betty was in church listening to Pastor Paul. After the service, Betty prepared lunch, all the while thinking about the conversations she had yesterday with family members at the reunion. She loved seeing them, but the conversations were always the same, stirring up both fond and agonizing memories. Jake felt the same way and was extremely wary and protective of what Jessie might hear.

As they sat down for lunch, Jake asked curiously, "What did you and your cousins talk about at the park yesterday?"

"Mostly school and the Olympics," said Jessie. "Linda and I are both starting seventh grade this year. She thinks it's going to be hard changing classrooms and teachers, but Steven said not to worry. It's very easy. Anyway, I don't think I'm going to have any problem. I'm looking forward to changing classrooms. That way, it won't be so boring."

"What about the Olympics?" asked Jake, trying to keep the conversation going. "Did we win the most medals? I did hear we won the men's downhill ski race. I think that was a big surprise."

"I'm not sure who won the most medals," replied Jessie. "We were discussing where the games were played. Did you know they were held in Yugoslavia this year? I didn't realize it was a communist country until Mr. Randall told us about it in school. Steven said his dad didn't think it was right for us to play in the games there but that he personally didn't have a problem with it. Mr. Randall told us every country should take its turn hosting the Olympic games, which would help make the world a better place. I like the idea; it makes sense to me. How about you, do you think that's right?"

"What do I think? I think the games should be about the athletes and not the country," stated Jake. "Finding out who the best athlete in the world is at what they do. Isn't that what the original Olympics were all about? It shouldn't make a difference what country is hosting the games. What else did you talk about?"

"Steven asked if we knew anyone hurt or killed in that Lebanon bombing last October," replied Jessie. "I didn't even know where Lebanon was or what he was talking about; I felt kind of stupid. Did you know about that? He said there were 200 American soldiers killed, maybe more. Is that correct?"

"Yes, I heard about it, and yes, it was very terrible," exclaimed Jake, as his voice grew louder. "We shouldn't have been there. Why we put our soldiers in harm's way, I will never understand. Sometimes, I think our elected officials have rocks in their heads."

Betty said calmly, "It's okay, don't get excited, Jake. She's just curious and needs to understand. They were there to keep peace, Pumpkin, to prevent a war from erupting in the region."

"That is exactly the problem," said Jake. "Everyone expects us to be the world police, to keep order. When is that going to stop?"

"Why would there be a war over there? Why would they want to bomb us if we were trying to keep peace?" asked Jessie in a worrisome tone.

Betty chimed in, "It's very difficult to understand why people do what they do. Some people think it's about religious differences, some think it's geopolitical, while others think that it's manifested in the seven deadly sins."

"What are they?" asked Jessie.

"Well, Pastor Paul describes them as greed, pride, wrath, envy, lust, gluttony, and sloth," answered Betty.

"Maybe they do need police to keep the peace," thought Jessie. "We have police here so people won't break the law. Wouldn't that be a good idea?"

"It's much more difficult than that," said Betty. "History has not been kind to that region. They say there are no winners in war, and that may be true, but I can tell you for sure that there are definitely losers. After the big wars, the Middle East was divided, and borders were redrawn. Many of those countries became colonies, causing tension and conflict between Arab and Western countries. I'm sure you will learn more in your high school history classes."

Jessie didn't know exactly what to think. They had never discussed world affairs, the seven deadly sins, or geopolitics, whatever that was, in elementary school. She began to realize just how little she knew about the world.

Jake was growing frustrated with the conversation and responded by saying, "It's all about oil. Whoever controls the oil controls the world. That's what it's all about."

"Does Vietnam have oil?" asked Jessie, searching for answers. "Is that why we were there?"

Jessie's question caught Jake off guard. *How did we get here?* He thought.

"No," answered Betty with a sigh. "I don't think so; that was completely different. Vietnam was at war with France for its independence before splitting into two separate countries. We were there to stop North Vietnam from spreading communism to the south."

Jake was ready to lose his temper. "Communism… shit! They called it a police action, but it was a war, an illegal war, waged without congressional approval. Our government lied to us and sent half a million soldiers there, and we know how that turned out… don't we?" Jake threw back his chair and left the room steaming, he had enough of that conversation.

Jessie fought back the tears. She had never seen her uncle lose his temper like that, and it was quite upsetting. "What did I say wrong, Grandma?"

"Nothing, Pumpkin, you said nothing wrong." Betty consoled Jessie, telling her how hard it was for Jake to have these conversations, what with John's death. "He will be okay in a bit after he settles down. You know, he's very protective of you; he loves you more than you can ever imagine. He doesn't realize how grown up you've become. I think that maybe you should go to work with your uncle tomorrow. I'll talk to him."

Chapter 7

Answers

Jake was happy to have Jessie tag along, especially after losing his temper in the kitchen the day before. He had grown very comfortable with her presence at work every day during the school year and missed those mornings and afternoons they spent together. Three weeks had passed since the start of summer break, and this was the first time Jessie would be back in the store.

Jessie was also delighted about spending the day with her uncle since Jimmy and Oscar were both grounded for a couple of days. Apparently, Oscar had left his bike behind the truck and his dad backed up over it, and because Jimmy was watching over him, they were both grounded for two days. Jessie didn't think that was very fair, but there was nothing she could do about it.

After unlocking the front doors and turning on the lights in the main store, Jake made his way to the back through the warehouse to raise the roll-up, bay doors. The time was 7:30, and the store was officially open. Bob wouldn't show up until nine o'clock as he stayed later into the evening to finish the books. While Jake was taking care of operations inside, Jessie pushed out the merchandise displayed in front: three push mowers, two Adirondack chairs, and a small pallet of bird seed.

At 8:45, Jake needed to leave and deliver a new John

Deere mower to Mr. Delong. Normally, Jake would wait until Bob arrived before leaving, but Mr. Delong was adamant that he needed the tractor before ten.

"Hey Jessie," shouted Jake, "I've got to take this mower over to Mr. Delong's place. Can you watch the store until Bob shows up? It should be no more than 15 or 20 minutes."

"What if a customer comes in?" Jessie asked. "What do I do?"

"You'll be fine. Just help them find whatever they need. You know where everything is. Tell them Bob will be here in a few minutes."

"Okay, can do," she replied confidently. She thought, *Wow, this is the first time he ever left me in charge,* and that made her feel particularly good, even grown up.

Ten minutes after Jake left for the delivery, Bob Fleming came through the door asking, "Where's Jake at? Did he quit or just run away?"

"No," laughed Jessie. "He left a few minutes ago taking a mower out to Mr. Delong's place, said he'd be back about 10:30 or so."

"Nice, what have you been up to this summer? I haven't seen you in nearly three weeks, and I swear you get taller every time I see you."

"Mostly hanging out with Jimmy and Oscar, our new neighbors. Do you know them?"

"I've seen them in the store with their dad. I knew their grandpa, although he was a few years older than me."

"You probably know everyone, don't you, Mr. Fleming?"

With a big smile, he said, "It does seem that way, doesn't

it."

"Did you know my dad?"

"Of course I did," said Bob reminiscently. "He and Richard were in school together, although Richard was a little older. Anyway, Roy brought him by the store all the time back then. He was a good boy, big and strong. You know, they were all good boys back then."

"You mean before the war?"

"Yes," he said solemnly. "That's exactly what I mean… before the war."

"Can you tell me about him?" asked Jessie, anxious to hear more.

"Well, let me see…I remember when Roy came back from Millsburg after Betty gave birth. Oh, he was oh so proud. It was his first child, and it was a boy. He couldn't have asked for more than that. He was still working the farm with his dad at that time; I think it was 1950 or 1951. I remember it was summer, a very hot summer that year. Anyway, John was always the best in Roy's eyes; he could do no wrong. He and Richard hung out together whenever he wasn't busy working on the farm. They liked playing basketball together, and John, well, he was very good. In fact, he was on the high school basketball team. As I recall, he wore the number 2 on the back of his jersey. I remember Roy going to every one of his games and coming into the store the following day telling me how many baskets John made. He was extremely proud."

"Was my father like Uncle Jake?" asked Jessie.

"How do you mean?"

"Well, my Uncle Jake can be funny sometimes, but he's

not very open. He doesn't like to talk about things, especially my father or my mother, and he gets mad when I ask questions or try to talk about the war."

"Your Uncle Jake adored John. He was his big brother, someone he looked up to, someone he could lean on and show him the way." His death was devastating.

"Did my uncle date my mother before she married my dad?"

"I suppose that's possible. They were all inseparable at that age. You would have to ask your uncle that question; I'm not sure. Anyway, you asked about your father, and I can tell you he was more outgoing than Jake, and all the girls loved him. He was good looking, athletic, and always the leader of the group. John liked being the center of attention, whether it was at school, playing basketball, or being in the church play, and he really loved life."

"My father went to church?" she asked in surprise.

"He sure did. Roy, Betty, John, and Jake all went. Every Sunday, they would be there at church taking in the service and listening to Pastor Paul."

"I don't think I've ever seen Uncle Jake go to church."

"You must understand, Jake took John's death extremely hard, as we all did; he idolized John, and then on the day of his burial, Roy had his heart attack and stroke. I can't even imagine what Jake and your family went through. It was a real tragedy. You know, the effects of war can be far-reaching, Jessie. Some casualties of war are not even on the battlefield but in the homes of those who served, and their families… well, they are often victims of war." Bob paused and looked at Jessie, wondering if she really understood. "Your Uncle Jake is a good person, and he just needed to sort things out. The war took his brother from him, and the church wasn't going to bring him back as far as he was concerned."

"Grandma goes to church service every Sunday, and she always comes home feeling refreshed. I pray my Uncle Jake will be happy, but I think he's still sad."

"All that I can say is that some people take great comfort in their faith and church. Religion is a very personal issue, and it is up to the person to decide what is right for them. Anyway, I probably shouldn't talk about church. I will say that your dad was a good man and part of our community before he died in Vietnam. Your Uncle Jake is also a good man."

"Thank you, Mr. Fleming, for talking about my dad and my uncle. I appreciate it."

"You're welcome. Hey, how about a pop? Here are some quarters; can you get us both a Coke-a-Cola from that machine over there?"

With a big grin, Jessie said, "Sure thing!" A cold Coke-a-Cola in a glass bottle on a summer day, who doesn't like that!

A couple of hours later, Jake came through the back after returning from delivering the mower. "I see how you both are," he said with a smile. "I'm working my butt off, and you two are having a party. Where's mine?"

"It's staying cold, Uncle Jake." She laughed while eyeing Mr. Fleming.

The afternoon passed without incident. Jake received inbound supplies and took care of the warehouse. Mr.

Fleming put Jessie to work organizing the hardware bins, ensuring all the nuts and bolts, washers, and cotter pins were in the correct bins.

On the drive home, Jake needed to get yesterday's episode off his chest. He hated himself for throwing his chair back and raising his voice in front of Jessie. That was not how he was raised, and he felt embarrassed about the whole situation.

"I'm sorry if I upset you yesterday," he said as his thoughts flashed back and forth between 1971 and the present. "I was terribly angry when John died – angry with him, angry that he left home, angry with our government. You would think after thirteen years, I could find peace, but I can't. I still hold that anger inside; I still see that Army staff car driving slowly down the lane, and I can still hear those words, 'We regret to inform you...' Anyway, it's my fault. I never should have said those words to him. I'm sorry."

Jessie was a little confused and didn't know exactly what to say. She just reached over, took his hand in hers, and held it tightly until they were home.

Chapter 8

Summer Fun

Going to work with Uncle Jake and talking with Mr. Fleming was nice, but summer vacation was for fun, and there was lots of that to be had. Unless Uncle Jake or Betty assigned her specific chores to do, Jessie had the run of the farm from sunrise to sunset. As long as she checked in occasionally and was not late for dinner, she and Shad had free reign to play and explore their world, which included the wooded areas on either side of the farm all the way to the lake and everything in between. This was her home, and she knew it like the back of her hand.

As much as Jessie enjoyed riding her bike around the farm, she, Jimmy, Oscar, and Shad, had plans for the day to hike through the woods and down to the lake to test their skills at fishing. The trip through the woods would take them along a six-foot wide path whittled out of the trees years earlier for snowmobiles. They had planned this trip for a while, and today would be perfect, with temperatures near 80 degrees, maybe 72 degrees, along the lake. Jimmy and Oscar cleared it with their mom the day before, and Betty made sandwiches for everyone to take. Before retrieving the fishing poles and gear from the garage, Jessie and Shad walked next door to see if the boys were ready.

The door to the Jenkins place opened upon knocking, and Jessie found herself looking directly at Jimmy's mom on the other side of the door for the first time. She thought, "How young and pretty," before introducing herself. "Hello, Mrs. Jenkins, I'm Jessie Peabody from next door. Are Jimmy and Oscar ready?

"You mean Brian."

"Oh, yeah!" exclaimed Jessie.

Mrs. Jenkins laughed. "They're almost ready; they need to finish making their beds. Come on in, you can wait inside. You know, I've been waiting for a chance to meet this girl named Jessie who has captivated my boys," she said playfully. "Now I know why... you are a ray of sunshine."

"We just like playing and hanging out together," said Jessie innocently. "We hope to catch some fish today."

"How are you and my boys getting to the lake?"

"Oh, it's very easy. We just walk east toward the lake, and there it is. It will only take us about 20 minutes."

"Can you be more precise than that? I'm not so familiar with this area."

"Sure, we will walk down the edge of the tree line until we pass the hedgerow at the end of this cornfield. Then, we will bear right onto the snowmobile path that goes through the woods all the way down to the lake. That will bring us out on Lake Road, and from there, we cross over to the lake. It's very nice there."

"Okay, I'm sure it's lovely there, but I don't want Jimmy or Oscar swimming in the lake, please. They both know how to swim, but their father says that the water is too cold. Can I trust you on that?" she asked openly.

"Of course," replied Jessie. "My Uncle Jake doesn't like

me swimming in the lake either, and you are right. It is very cold."

The boys finished making their beds, combing their hair, and brushing their teeth and were ready to exit the house when Mrs. Jenkins knelt down and gave them both a big kiss and a hug and said, "You be safe now. No swimming."

Both Jimmy and Oscar said, "Okay, we know," at the exact same time, as though they had rehearsed that answer a hundred times.

Jessie added, "We'll be back by two o'clock, Mrs. Jenkins. I need to help my grandma later," and off they went.

After a brief stop by the farm to pick up poles, fishing gear, and sandwiches, they set out on their delightful journey, all three wearing cutoff jeans, T-shirts, and sneakers. Hiking down to the lake was a first for the boys and the furthest they had wandered from their house since moving in. From the farmhouse, they passed the old shed and made their way along the hedgerow to the tree line, where they picked up the path that led to the lake.

The view from the hedgerow was amazing; they could see the cornfields stretch out across the lower farm with Lake Tiohero in the background. There wasn't a stitch of clouds in the sky, giving the lake the appearance of a blue diamond shimmering in the distance.

"Wow, that's beautiful!" said Oscar as he brought up the rear.

"I didn't realize you could see the lake from here," Jimmy added. "You are so lucky. I wish we could see it from our house."

I surely am, she thought knowingly.

As they left the fields and entered the woods, their world changed abruptly. The trees were full of leaves in the middle of July, blocking out much of the sun making it somewhat cooler and darker. A more earthly, musty scent of decaying leaves from past years filled the air, and there were so many new sounds – leaves rustling, twigs breaking, acorns dropping, squirrels scurrying around leaping from tree to tree, and Snyder Creak trickling in the background as it meandered downward toward the lake. Their world was alive, and they could see, feel, hear, and smell it as they strolled along the path. There was so much to take in; the boys hardly spoke a word. Jessie spent the time reflecting on what she had learned so far about her parents but suspected there must be more to the story. Before they knew it, they had reached the lake road at the end of the path.

Jessie smiled, "Okay, we're here. We just need to cross the road; there are some steps leading down to the lake right over there," as she pointed to the left. "Follow me."

Shad wasn't about to follow anyone. He was already across the road and heading for the water. Maybe the kids couldn't go swimming, but that didn't stop him. Of course, there's just no way of keeping a golden retriever out of the water.

As Shad splashed around, the three made their way down the steps and onto a cement foundation that reached out into the water. What used to be a lakefront cabin was now a place for them to sit and drop their lines in hopes of catching something. The cabin had burnt down decades earlier, and the only remnant left was the foundation from which they dangled their feet. The depth of the water below their feet was about four feet, and there was no sandy beach; there were just rocks and pebbles.

"What do you think," Jimmy asked, "are we going to get lucky?"

"I'm going to catch a big one; just wait and see!" said Oscar, his eyes gleaming with anticipation.

"I bet you I will get a bigger one than you," replied Jimmy as he cast his line out as far as he could.

Jessie laughed. "I think we will be extremely lucky if we catch anything." To her, it really wasn't about fishing; it was about sitting there in her beautiful world, at the edge of the lake, and spending time with friends. "It was nice meeting your mom this morning. I think she's really pretty and nice. You guys are really lucky."

Oscar then asked innocently, "Why do you live on the farm with your Uncle Jake and grandparents?"

"I've always lived here on the farm. It's my home," said Jessie. "Uncle Jake, Grandma, Grandpa, and Shad, they are my family."

Jimmy told Oscar he shouldn't ask such questions, to which Oscar replied, "I just wondered about her parents."

"It's okay," said Jessie. "My dad died before I was born, and my mom died in the hospital after having me. I never knew either one of them, although I do wonder what they were like. I've only known my uncle and grandparents."

"How did they die?" asked Jimmy.

"Well, neither my uncle nor grandma talks about it much. All that I know is my dad was in the army, and he died in Vietnam. They said my mom died of complications, but I really don't know what that means. What about your dad? Was he in the army?"

"No, not that I know of anyway," said Jimmy. "He said he went to school at Millsburg College, and that's where he met our mother. She was from the city."

"What does your dad do?" asked Jessie.

"He's a professor now at Millsburg College. He teaches history there and says it's the greatest job in the world."

"Does your mom work?"

Not yet, but she's going to be teaching fourth grade this year at Cayuga Falls Elementary School," said Jimmy proudly. "She's an excellent teacher."

Jessie's thoughts returned to fourth grade for an instant as she saw herself standing there, in front of Mr. Atkinson's desk, holding those books in hand with her arms extended and thinking, "I will never rid myself of this memory."

Then, out of nowhere, the memory was gone in a flash as her fishing line tightened with a quick, firm tug on the pole. "I've got a bite!" she proclaimed with a big grin on her face. "Get the net, Oscar, hurry, give it to Jimmy!"

"Don't let it get away," shouted Oscar.

Shad was barking with excitement.

"Jimmy, get ready."

Jessie started reeling in the line, and within seconds, they could see something jumping and splashing in the water about fifteen feet from where they sat. It was a small lake trout giving its best to put up a fight, but today, Jessie would win. Oscar handed the net to Jimmy, who laid flat on the cement, leaning over the edge. With one swoop, he was able to capture the prize, a 25-inch lake trout weighing about six pounds.

Jimmy asked Jessie if she would like him to take the hook out, but Jessie declined, saying, "No, I've got it; Uncle Jake showed me how to do it." She thought *He's going to be so proud of me today.*

After all that excitement of snagging the fish, it was time for lunch. Grandma, who wasn't sure what the boys would like, made a variety of sandwiches: two ham and cheese, one bologna and cheese, and one peanut butter. She also threw in an apple for each of them. When they finished, they all laid there on their backs looking up at the sky, which was now partly sunny, each laughing, pointing out different clouds that seemed to take on a life of their own. One looked like a cat, another a genie, and yet another a cartoon character. Without a worry in the world, they laid there with a sense of peacefulness, listening to the small waves break against the pebble beach.

They had been at the lake for a couple of hours, and it was now time to leave and make their way back uphill to the farm. Jessie had promised Mrs. Jenkins she would have the boys back by two o'clock, and she always kept her promises. The boys were in no hurry to leave, however. This was pure heaven to them, and like all children, they could not resist the temptation to remove their sneakers and stick their feet in the water.

Oscar cringed and screamed, "Oh my gosh, this is freezing!"

Jimmy laughed. "How can anyone swim in this water? It's too cold!"

Jessie watched while the boys splashed around for a few

minutes. "You should probably get out before your feet turn blue and fall off."

"Really?" said Oscar with a frightening look.

Jimmy and Jessie laughed before Oscar realized she was just kidding.

"That's not funny," he said.

The time was a little past one when they crossed the road to begin their trek back up the hill. The trip only took twenty minutes coming down but would take at least thirty minutes for them going up with gravity playing a big part in that. They were each in their own little worlds as they made their way uphill and through the woods, each tired from a day in the sun. Jessie's thoughts returned to her Uncle Jake dating her mother, as Lori Palmer claimed. She needed clarity but felt those closest to her were being tight-lipped about that relationship, and that made her suspicious. Asking her uncle, however, was out of the question; she needed to find another way.

As they came out of the woods, they turned right, making their way along the hedgerow and past the shed before arriving at the garage. First, they would put away the poles and fishing gear, then go inside and present Grandma with their trophy.

She was astounded; catching a fish was very unusual for Jessie, let alone a nice lake trout. "Oh, Pumpkin, that is so nice. Your Uncle Jake is going to be proud of you. Let me get the Polaroid camera and take a picture of you all holding the fish…That is going to be a great picture."

"What should I do with the fish, Grandma?"

"Just leave it in the pail there; I will take care of it."

"Okay," Jessie replied, "I'm going to walk Jimmy and Oscar back to their house. I will be back shortly." The three of them and Shad trudged off to cross Snyder Creek one more time.

Chapter 9

Restoration

The following morning at the breakfast table, Jessie looked at her grandpa and said, "Mr. Fleming said my dad was a really good basketball player. I didn't know… but I was thinking, Uncle Jake, there's a basketball hoop and a backboard in the barn. I would like to play there if you could fix it up for me. The rim is bent a little, and it doesn't have a net. I will also need a basketball."

Betty piped in, saying, "I think that is a great idea; what do you think, Jake? You boys played there all the time while you were growing up."

Even Roy showed his approval by nodding his head slightly and mumbling.

Jake agreed. "Yeah, of course, I can fix it up for you. We'll go down to Millsburg after our diner run on Saturday morning and buy you a new net and basketball. We can probably find those at Sears and Roebuck. Right now, I've got to get to work. I think that barn is going to need a little straightening up if you want to play there."

Jessie was thrilled and, with a radiant smile, said, "Maybe I'll be good enough to make the basketball team like my dad."

"Pumpkin, you can be whatever you desire if you put your mind to it," answered Betty. "You just have to work at it."

With that said, Jake left for work, Betty started clearing the breakfast table, and Roy retreated to the sitting room. Jessie's mind focused on the barn and straightening it up as her Uncle Jake had said. She would enlist the help of her two friends from across Snyder Creek; after all, they would be playing there and shooting baskets as well. "This is going to be great," she thought.

Before heading over to the Jenkins house to recruit the boys, she would first survey the project at hand. Located just a few hundred feet on the other side of the garage, the barn sat on the crest, dividing the upper and lower parts of the farm. She thought it was quite ingenious how they positioned the barn in that exact spot. From the east side, they could drive tractors and equipment directly into the lower floor or basement dug out of the crest as it sloped down toward the lake. From both the south and the west sides, the upper or first floor was accessible straight on through large sliding doors as its elevation was the same as the surrounding fields. The barn also had a loft at the north end for storing hey, but that had been empty for as long as she could remember.

As she slid open the large sliding door facing the house, light filtered in, and she could see the entirety of the upper floor. She could also see sunlit rays beaming through the cracks and streaming down, creating slivers of light on the large plank floor laid out in front of her. There, centered on the east wall, was the basketball hoop and backboard. As she looked closely, she could still make out faint lines painted on the floor some twenty years earlier. Standing there with her hands on her hips, she had visions of bringing this basketball court back to life. It really wouldn't take a lot of work. There was a pile of leftover lumber that needed to be moved and restacked underneath the hayloft, and it definitely needed a good sweeping as the floor hadn't been touched in years. With a little TLC, a touch of paint, and a new net, it would be ready for a game.

The time had come to fetch Jimmy and Oscar and begin the restoration process. Jessie closed the barn door and raced to the garage for her bike. She needed a couple of tries with the kick-starter this morning before the engine fired up and reached a steady idle. Soon, she was off racing down the lane and along the road to Snyder Creek. She would make a couple of trips around the field before stopping at the corner of the property where Jimmy and Oscar were waiting to ask, "What's up?"

"Do you like to play basketball?" asked Jessie.

"I do," responded Oscar.

Jimmy acknowledged likewise.

"Good, my Uncle Jake is going to fix the basketball rim in the barn so we can play there. It needs straightening up a little bit, and I could use your help. Can you give me a hand... do you have time?"

"Sure, let me ask Mom," replied Jimmy, "Give me a minute." He could be heard yelling as he began jogging back to the house, "Mom, Oscar, and I are going over to Jessie's house for a while. Is that okay?"

Mrs. Jenkins replied, "Be back by noon."

The three of them spent the rest of the morning clearing the court, restacking the lumber in the corner under the hayloft, and sweeping out the barn. The floor needed sweeping three times, and they needed to take several breaks as the dust became too thick in the air for them to breathe. Finally, they gave the floor a good hosing down before calling it quits, letting everything dry out.

This was the first time both Jimmy and Oscar had the opportunity to see the inside of a barn. They were taken back by the sheer size of the timbers, rafters, and joist holding the structure upright, not to mention how much space there was inside. Jessie gave them a complete tour from the lower basement, which was full of farm equipment used by Mr. Jacobs, to the empty hayloft above, which her uncle forbid her to climb up, as it had no guardrails.

As they left, Jessie asked, "Are you coming over tomorrow so we can finish?"

Oscar questioned what they needed to do. "I thought we were done?"

"I want to repaint those lines on the floor. I'm sure Uncle Jake has some paint in the garage. He has everything else."

"I'll help you, Jessie. I don't have anything to do tomorrow," replied Jimmy, who was beginning to enjoy the time they spent together.

"Excellent, I will scrounge up everything we need," Jessie said. "This is going to be the best, just wait and see!"

Her enthusiasm and passion were obvious and contagious; you could see it in her eyes, hear it in her voice, and feel it in her energy. Jimmy was beginning to understand what his mother meant when she said, "You are a ray of sunshine."

After lunch, Jessie went to the garage in search of supplies needed to finish the project they started. She was sure Uncle Jake had some paint left over from when he painted the barn two summers ago. First, she would look in the metal locker where he kept most liquids. "Let's see," she said to herself as she shuffled through the items, "10W-30 Motor Oil, antifreeze, WD-40, starting fluid, a coffee can containing some gas with a couple of paint brushes, this might due. Hmm, I wonder where he put the paint, possibly under the workbench."

Jake kept his garage organized, with many of his tools hanging from the pegboard mounted above the bench, each with a painted silhouette behind it. Jessie helped her uncle enough to know the names of all the tools and their uses. In the cabinet under the bench, she found what she was looking for. There, in a white cardboard box, were three unopened one-gallon cans of paint, one white and two red. *This would have to do,* she thought. As she pulled the cans of paint from beneath the cabinet, a small cardboard box fell out to the side and opened. *What's this, pictures, cards and letters?* As she began sorting through the contents, she realized they were there for a purpose, set aside as a keepsake, meant to be private.

She thought it best to put everything back under the cabinet, including the small box; however, her curiosity got the best of her, and she could not resist examining its contents further. The best place to do that would be in her room, at night, after everyone went to bed. After tidying up the cabinet beneath the workbench, she concealed the small box under her arm and went straight to her room, putting it and its secrets in the nightstand next to her bed.

Later that evening, after everyone retired to their rooms,

Jessie laid in bed with a flashlight, studying the contents of her newly found treasure. There were several news articles cut out from the local newspaper, mostly about her dad being captain of the basketball team and how many points he scored during the games. Then there were two other articles, one relating to his service in the Army with a picture of his graduation from basic training, the other about his marriage announcement to Mary. The most interesting items she found were two Polaroid pictures of Jake, one with him and Emily from his junior prom and the second with him and Mary at his senior prom. There was also a cute card from Mary to Jake stating what a wonderful time she had that night. As she drifted off to sleep, she tried to imagine what it must have been like back then, prior to her mom and dad being married, prior to her birth.

The following morning, Jimmy returned to lend Jessie a hand, this time without Oscar, who was not feeling well. He probably inhaled too much dust during the sweeping process the prior day. Jessie was outside with a tennis ball, playing catch with Shad, eagerly awaiting her partner. She had already taken a couple of paintbrushes and a gallon of each color over to the barn earlier that morning after Jake left for work.

"Can you help me with the door," asked Jessie. "It sticks sometimes."

"Sure, watch out, I'll get it for you," he said as he put his shoulder into it and gave it a mighty push.

Upon surveying the floor, Jessie said she thought it was dry enough from yesterday's hosing down to begin painting.

"Yeah, I think you're right," agreed Jimmy, "It looks good to me."

"There's a screwdriver over there by the gallon of white paint – can you open it, please, and give it a stir with that paint stick?" she asked. "I'm going to look for a small board to use as a straightedge since we don't have any tape."

"What's the red paint for?" asked Jimmy.

Jessie was waiting for him to ask. "You can paint that area between the free throw line and the wall beneath the backboard red. That section is referred to as the paint in basketball terminology."

Painting the various boundary lines and free throw area took them all morning, but they were very careful not to spill any paint on the court or themselves. When they finished, they stood back and admired their work; with a little imagination, it looked like the real thing.

Jimmy said, "I can't wait to play a game."

"Me too," replied Jessie. "Mr. Fleming told me my dad was really good and played on the high school basketball team. I want to do the same."

"Does our school even have a girls' junior high basketball team?" asked Jimmy inquisitively.

That possibility hadn't crossed her mind, and just the thought of not having the opportunity to play riled her. *I'll play on the boys' team if I have to*, she thought.

That evening after dinner, while helping with the dishes, Jessie asked Betty if she could sew a number 2 on the back of one of her old T-shirts.

"Whatever for?" she asked.

"Mr. Fleming told me that was my father's number

when he played on the high school basketball team.”

“Is that right?” Betty thought for a moment. “I think I might be able to come up with something; wait here, Pumpkin.” When she returned, she was holding a white jersey with gold and black trim down both sides and around the sleeves. On the back was the number 2 with the name PEABODY in bold letters.

“I don’t know why I kept this all these years,” she said, crying, “but I think he would like you to have it.”

Jessie was speechless, with a lump growing in her throat and tears in her eyes, she gave her grandma a warm and lasting hug.

Saturday finally came and Jake yelled upstairs for Jessie, “It’s time to go to the diner. Are you coming?”

“I’ll be right down, don’t leave.”

To Jake’s surprise, Jessie came running into the kitchen wearing a Cayuga Falls HS home basketball jersey with the number 2 and her name on the back.

“Where did you get that?” he asked as he looked over at Betty.

“Where do you think?” said Betty. “Don’t you remember… that was the jersey John wore in high school? I found it with some other things in my closet. It only needed a tuck here and there and hemmed up a bit. I think it fits her pretty well.”

“Wow, looking good; I guess we better go get you that basketball and net so you can show me what you got. I’m hungry; let’s stop by the diner first before we drive all the way to Millsburg.”

Jake had other reasons for wanting to stop by the diner.

He hadn't seen Emily all week and wanted to make sure they were still on for Friday night. Memories of years past were still swirling around inside of him, and he was looking forward to taking her to the carnival and where that might lead.

Jessie had her own reasons for going to the diner other than the normal Saturday ritual. She discovered parts of the past, her roots, and her identity, and she wanted to show it off by wearing her father's old jersey.

Chapter 10

Carnival

The three musketeers and Shad spent much of the week playing basketball and traipsing around the farm. By Wednesday evening, all the carnies had arrived in town with their trucks, tents, rides, booths, and games in preparation for the big show starting the following evening and lasting throughout the weekend. They would set up at the fairgrounds, which was nothing more than an open field with some bleachers and a small building used for administration and ticket sales. On the backside of that building were four washrooms for everyone's convenience.

Thursday came, and Betty drove into town for her weekly grocery shopping. This was the one and only day of the week that she would find herself behind the wheel of her car, and that was only because Jake was at work. She never enjoyed driving and, over the years, had grown accustomed to being chauffeured around, first by Roy, then John, and now, of course, Jake. Jessie was by her side, grabbing the needed items off the shelves as Betty marked them off her list.

Since the IGA was the only grocery store in town, everyone shopping there usually knew everyone else, and that provided a perfect opportunity to catch up on the latest happenings around town. Jake always said it was nothing more than gossip, but Betty took offense, reminding him that his trips to the diner every Saturday morning were no different. Jessie enjoyed going to both places and appreciated the conversations and information shared by all helping her to assess the world around her. Most of the conversations that day concerned the carnies arriving and roaming the streets of town along with opening night festivities. There was an air of excitement in Cayuga Falls preceding the once-in-a-year event.

When the shopping was finished and the groceries loaded in the car, Jessie asked eagerly, "Can we drive up West End Road and check out the carnival?"

Betty replied, "Of course, Pumpkin. I'm also curious to see what it looks like. You know, I haven't been to one of these carnivals in… I don't know how many years. It's been a long time, for sure."

"Why don't you go, Grandma? It's a lot of fun."

"I don't know. I'm not much on those rides, they always made me dizzy. To tell you the truth, I can't say that I ever found any value in going there. We didn't have a lot of extra money when the boys were growing up, and we were forever working the farm."

"Look, there it is. Oh, wow! Check out the Ferris wheel. It's gigantic!" exclaimed Jessie.

"I'm afraid of those – you won't catch me riding on that thing."

"I can't wait until tomorrow night. Jimmy said his mom and dad were considering going and, if so, would take both him and Oscar. It's going to be so much fun."

Jessie was amazed at how fast the carnies assembled the rides and booths, turning the empty fairgrounds into an amusement park in less than a day. She didn't notice all the necessary work that was still going on, like setting up generators, stringing lights and cables, and inspecting the rides. It would take the rest of the afternoon and loads of hard work before the carnival was ready to open.

The rest of the day saw Betty putting away the groceries and making dinner, Roy sitting in his chair watching TV, Jessie riding her bike around the farm, and Jake finishing up working with Bob. Jimmy and Oscar were playing outside. Mrs. Jenkins was working on household chores while Mr. Jenkins was working next semester's syllabus. Emily Jacobs was finishing her shift at the diner and would soon be heading home, but first, she would stop by the Feed & Seed to visit with Jake.

After a brief conversation with Bob at the counter, Emily walked to the back of the store.

"What's going on, Jake?"

"Oh, not much; I'm just finishing stacking all this seed that was delivered this morning," he replied, wiping away the sweat from his brow. "It's a warm one today."

"Would you like me to get you a glass of water or something?" asked Emily nicely.

"No, I'm good. What brings you over here?"

"Well, you didn't exactly say what time you were picking me up tomorrow or if we were just meeting up at the fairgrounds."

Jake looked at her. "No, I'll pick you up… Is this a date?"

"That would be fine with me. I mean, if you're good with that," she said, trying to be coy.

"Well, the reason I ask is because I promised Jessie that I would take her to the carnival. I was hoping the three of us could go together. I wasn't sure how you might feel about that."

"Jake, do you think I'm that shallow? Of course, Jessie can come with us; besides, I really like her, maybe even more than you," she added with a smirk.

Jake looked a little dismayed, "Okay, I get it."

Emily gave Jake a quick peck on the cheek before running off. "You can pick me up at seven tomorrow night."

Jake felt like he was sixteen again when Emily gave him that kiss, not so different from the first time she had kissed him. Did she mean it as a friendly, polite gesture, or did she mean it as more than that? That question would linger in his thoughts, haunting him for the rest of the day.

Jake left work at the usual time Friday evening and headed straight to the house with Emily on his mind. The boys had already left the farm after an afternoon of playing basketball in the barn with Jessie. Everyone would spend the next couple of hours having dinner and preparing to go out for a night of fun at the carnival.

The drive over to Seth Jacob's place to pick up Emily was a short five minutes for Jake and Jessie. As they left, Betty gave Jake a hug and a smile. "Have a good time, you look good." She then looked at Jessie. "You too, Pumpkin, be safe and hang on tight if you go on those rides."

After getting in the truck, Jessie noticed Jake had put on some cologne and snickered, "What's that smell, Uncle Jake?"

"That's Old Spice," Jake replied. "Why, do you think I put too much on?"

"No," she replied laughingly. "It's good, she will like it. I just never knew that you wore perfume."

"You mean cologne?"

Jessie blushed. "Oh, yeah."

When they reached the Jacobs house, Jake asked Jessie to stay in the truck while he went to check on Emily. Seth was sitting on the front porch smoking a pipe and cordially greeted Jake asking him what he thought of the corn this year, to which he replied, "Not bad, but we desperately need some rain soon if it's going to be a good harvest."

"Yeah, we definitely need some of that," said Seth. "Emily should be out in a few minutes, Jake. You know how women are."

Emily knew Jake was waiting out on the front porch with her father but would give them a couple of minutes to themselves before going out. When she did, she said, "Let's go; I'll see you later, Dad. Don't wait up." She was dressed casually in a blue denim skirt, a red-checkered blouse tied at the waist, and cowgirl boots, and she smelled of baby powder with a hint of jasmine.

Jake, being the gentleman that he was, opened the door for Emily as Jessie slid to the middle of the truck's bench seat. Through the open window, he said softly, "You look nice tonight." He then gave Seth a wave, got in the truck, and they were off to have a good time.

The gates at the fairgrounds opened at five, and by 7:30, the carnival was in full swing. In fact, the parking lot had reached full capacity, and they would need to park the truck two blocks down on West End Road and walk from there. On their journey to the grounds, they passed Mr. Jenkins' pickup and Jessie was relieved they had decided to go. She was now hoping to meet up with Jimmy and Oscar so they could enjoy the rides and games together, screaming, laughing, and joking around without being a stone around Jake and Emily's neck. Jessie was smart enough to know that he wanted to spend the evening with Emily, and she was happy to oblige.

Jake paid the entrance fees and bought a large roll of tickets for Jessie to use on the rides and games. Time had come for her to find the boys. The sun had just gone down, and dusk would soon give way to night. Then, with the flip of a switch, the lights strung throughout the fairgrounds illuminated, bringing the carnival to life. The oohs and ahhs grew louder mixing in with the jabbering, chattering, and mingling of children and adults alike. In the background, the melodic tune of carousel played nonstop along with the sounds of Carnies yelling "Step right up, a winner every time," and "Get your cotton candy" while soliciting participation in a search of their fortunes. This was their livelihood.

Jessie soon spotted the boys who were walking with their parents not far in front of them. She tugged at Jake's arm and said, "I'm going to join them if it's okay with you, Uncle Jake."

Jake replied, "Let's go see them first and see what they say."

Mr. Jenkins put out his hand, "How are you, Jake? It's been a long time; do you remember me?"

"I'm fine, thanks – it's Gene, right?" replied Jake. "Yeah, it has been a long time. I can't say I remember exactly when, though."

"I think I left for college while you were still in junior high," recalled Gene. "I was helping your dad out on the farm from time to time those last few summers while I was in high school. Oh yeah, where's my manners? This is my wife, Susan; I don't believe you've met her."

"Pleased to meet you," said Jake, looking at Susan. "That's right; you were a few years older than John. I remember you throwing those bales of hay in the loft while John stacked them neatly. Anyway, it's nice seeing you again."

It was now Jessie's turn to chime in. "Is it okay if I go on the rides with Jimmy and Oscar tonight… I mean Brian, Mrs. Jenkins?"

"Of course, you can join us, sweetie. If you wish, Jake, we could bring her home after the carnival. We're only planning to stay until 10:30, maybe eleven at the latest.

Jake looked at Emily for an answer, who looked back at him and said, "That's your decision."

Jake said he was okay, and Gene said, "Okay, it's a go."

Before going their separate ways, Jake reminded Jessie to be on her best behavior and mind her manners. This was nothing more than a formality, a habit left over from his upbringing, for he knew that Jessie would be polite and mindful. That was her nature.

Jessie felt a little nervous as she and her friends made their way from booth to booth, playing games and spending their tickets. Soon, however, she put that anxiety out of her mind. She particularly liked throwing the darts at the balloons, where she actually won a tiny stuffed bear the size of her palm. With the boys by her side, they were having the times of their lives as they stopped at each booth, if not to play, then just to watch everyone else having fun trying to win the big prize.

The crowd was large, so making one's way down game row toward the rides took some time. Along the way, they treated themselves to some pink cotton candy, enjoying the moment. Finally, there it was, right there in front of them, reaching high into the sky and spinning faster than they imagined was the Ferris wheel.

"Come on!" said Jimmy. "Let's get in line."

"Yeah, I want to ride on that," shouted Oscar, full of excitement. "I hope it stops on top for us. We should be able to see the whole town from up there."

With all the exhilaration, Jessie's nervous feeling returned and felt a little deeper and a little sharper than it felt earlier in the day. She recalled the conversation with her grandma the day before. *Maybe I shouldn't go on the ride,* she thought, and then, *I must go. I cannot lose face now, not in front of Jimmy and Oscar. What will they think? They will laugh and tease me, calling me a coward because I'm a girl. I will have to suck it up and ride this Ferris wheel no matter what.*

When it came time to board, Jimmy and Oscar slid to opposite sides of the seat, leaving the middle open for Jessie. It took several stops and goes, each making the seat rock back and forth, before the ride was completely full of screaming passengers. Oscar got his wish, and the Ferris wheel stopped with the three of them at its pinnacle, the seat swinging freely in the breeze and all three screaming.

Jessie felt dizzy and uncomfortable but tried not to let on. Instead of enjoying the ride as she so imagined, she could hardly wait for it to finish. For Jimmy and Oscar, it couldn't be sweeter; they were hoping it would last forever.

After planting her feet firmly on the ground and relieved when the ride was over, Jessie looked at Mrs. Jenkins and said, "I need to use the washroom. Is that okay?"

"Sure, would you like me to come with you?"

"No, that's okay," replied Jessie. "I'll be back in a few minutes."

On her way to the washrooms, Jessie spotted Jake and Emily standing with a crowd near the dance floor, listening to the band play county music. She decided she would stop and say hello since they were right there, but that was not the real reason. She wanted Emily's comfort and advice.

"Are you having fun, Uncle Jake? Have you two gone on any rides?"

"No, not yet," replied Jake. "What are you doing… where's the rest of your gang?"

Jessie pointed in the direction of the Ferris wheel and said, "They're over there, but I need to use the washroom." She then looked up at Emily with pleading eyes and asked, "Can you come with me?"

Emily looked at Jake. "We'll be back in a few minutes; us ladies need to freshen up. Come on, sweetie."

"Okay, I'll be right here listening to the music; hurry back."

By the time they reached the washroom, Jessie began to

cry softly. "I don't feel so well. I think I might have had an accident on the Ferris wheel; I feel a little strange."

"Don't you fret, sweetie; we've all been there before," replied Emily in a gentle and compassionate voice as she put her arm around Jessie's shoulders. "We'll freshen up and gather ourselves, and everything will be fine. Have you felt like this for very long?"

"No," she replied with a whimper, "It started earlier this afternoon. I had some cramps, but nothing bad. I thought I ate something that didn't agree with me."

"I think I have just what you need, sweetie." Emily understood the situation well and had already guessed what had happened before Jessie even realized it. She was happy to be there for her in her time of need and happy to watch her mature and grow into a beautiful young lady.

Jessie soon discovered that she did not have an accident after all; it was Mother Nature taking its course. She knew this day would come eventually but never gave it a second thought and was not prepared for it to happen, especially that day. Looking back, she now understood why she felt the way she did, that feeling below, the cramps, the dizziness, but regardless, she still felt embarrassed. After all she had been through, she was very grateful that Emily was there to confide in and comfort her in a motherly way.

After freshening up and catching their breath, they returned to find Jake standing in the same spot they left him. Emily looked at Jake, gave a slight tilt of the head, and said, "I think it's time for us to go; I'll explain later. Jessie, why don't you and I go tell Susan we are leaving?"

Jake was confused and, with a hint of sarcasm, said,

"Okay, I'll be right here until you get back, and then I guess we'll be leaving." He thought, *Damn, there goes the evening.* He felt the disappointment and sadness building inside and wondered if he would get another chance with Emily.

Chapter 11

Emily

The drive back to the farm, in the dead of night, only took twenty minutes, but that was long enough for Jessie to doze off against Emily's shoulder. When they arrived, Emily gave Jake a sweet smile and said, "Poor thing, I think she's asleep."

Jake gave her a soft nudge and said, "We're home. Come on, let's go inside; you've had a long day."

The house was quiet and mostly dark, with only the kitchen light left on. Betty and Roy had long since retired for the night, though Shad was there waiting faithfully by the back door with his tail wagging. Jake walked Jessie into the house, gave her a hug and a warm kiss on the head, and whispered, "Brush your teeth and go to bed; I'll be back after I take Emily home. Do you want me to wake you in the morning?"

"No, that's okay. I might sleep in tomorrow."

"Okay, that's fine, sleep tight."

Jake returned to the truck to a waiting Emily. The evening did not go exactly as he had planned, but now they had some time together alone. Emily slid to the middle of the seat to be near Jake as they made their way back to the Jacobs farm. He began apologizing for leaving the carnival early when Emily interrupted.

"Jake, do you even know why we left early? Do you

have any idea why Jessie felt the way she did?

"Because she wasn't feeling well. I'm guessing she ate too much cotton candy or something like that. Those things happen."

"Yeah, well, other things happen also, Jake. You should open your eyes. She's not that little baby girl anymore; she's growing and maturing. She's going through changes, and you need to be aware. I know you love her, but you need to be there for her, talk with her, comfort and support her, show her you care."

"You don't think I do those things?" asked Jake, feeling a little miffed. The evening was definitely not turning out as he planned.

"No, of course not; you are the best uncle Jessie could ever ask for. You're doing a great job bringing her up, and you're a better dad than most dads are. I'm just saying you need to pay more attention to her. Tonight, she had her first period, and you didn't even know."

Jake finally understood where Emily was coming from. "Damn… you're right. I didn't even realize. How can I be such a fool?"

Emily laughed and, with a smile, said, "Because you're a man, Jake… Listen, I had a good time tonight; Jessie will be fine. Maybe I'll come over after work tomorrow, and the two of us girls can go shopping. Do you think she would like that?"

What girl doesn't like to go shopping, Jake thought. "That will be fine, and I'm sure she will love that."

Emily took Jake's hand in hers, "Thank you for the evening; we should do this again. Will I see you at the diner in the morning?"

"I'll be there."

Before saying anything else, she leaned in, giving Jake a very long and passionate kiss, a kiss that left no doubt about her feelings. She then said, "Okay, I've got to get up early tomorrow; I'll see you then." She ran to the front porch and disappeared for the night.

The following morning, before heading off to the diner, Jake sat at the kitchen table with Betty and filled her in on the previous night's events. He told her how Jessie was upset and embarrassed having her menarche while she was with the boys at the carnival, and that led to them leaving early at ten o'clock to come home.

"Oh, I'm so sorry," said Betty. "Poor child, it's my fault. I should have prepared her better… I knew it was coming. What was I thinking?"

"It's okay, Mom, it's not all your fault," replied Jake. "I was completely unaware; hell, I didn't even think about it. Emily probably thinks I'm an idiot… she gave me an earful last night, but still, I was glad she was there. She was a huge comfort to Jessie. Anyway, I think I will head on over to the diner."

"Tell Emily I said hello and thank her for me, will you?"

"You can thank her yourself. She said she's coming over here after her shift and taking Jessie shopping with her in Millsburg this afternoon."

"She'll like that," said Betty as Jake went out the back door.

The time was a little past seven when Jake drove down the lane on his way into town. Betty sat there for a while, taking her time, drinking her coffee, and putting herself in Jessie's shoes, wondering, "What it's like growing up without a mother or father, being raised by an uncle and grandmother, and missing out on that paternal love and bond that comes instinctively." She knew that they had done their very best, but was that good enough? "Could we have done better?"

Shad sensing Betty's melancholy mood, rested his head in her lap and looked up at her with those big, brown, sad eyes before barking as if to say, "Okay, let's get moving."

Betty replied, "You're right. I need to quit feeling sorry for myself and get busy. I'll make Jessie some of her favorite pancakes."

Breakfast at the diner was great as usual, and Emily was full of smiles. She told Jake again that she had a wonderful time at the carnival and that she would come by the house around one o'clock to pick up Jessie. She also apologized for being a little harsh with him, saying, "I shouldn't have said those things to you last night, Jake. It wasn't my place, and you didn't deserve it. You're doing a fantastic job with Jessie. She loves you to no end, and I admire you for that."

Back at the farm, Jessie woke to the smell of coffee, pancakes, and bacon frying in a skillet. She felt far better this morning after sleeping in, something that she seldom did, and was hungry, so she skipped making her bed, got dressed, and made her way down the stairs and straight to the kitchen.

"Morning Pumpkin, you slept in today. Jake already went to the diner, so I made you your favorite."

"Thanks, Grandma!" said Jessie, looking hungry. "Are

we doing anything special today?"

"If I understood your Uncle Jake correctly, you and Emily are going shopping together in Millsburg this afternoon," replied Betty.

"No kidding, to the mall, just me and her? I haven't been there in forever. I think I only have about eight dollars," said Jessie.

"That's okay, Pumpkin; Jake gave me forty dollars to give you. He said you were growing and needed new clothes for the coming school year."

Jessie's eyes lit up as if it was Christmas. Going to the mall, buying new clothes, and shopping with Emily – could the day be any better? She was filled with anticipation.

Betty knew the excitement was building within Jessie – she could see it in her eyes and hear it in her voice – but she so wanted to ask her about last night. She couldn't seem to find the words or opportunity to ask the right question and was hoping Jessie might offer up the topic herself. That didn't happen, so Betty thought it best to give her a little time.

Emily finished her shift at noon, drove home, and had a quick bite to eat before driving over to the Peabody farm. When she arrived, Shad met her halfway to the back door, giving her a warm greeting. Betty opened the door, welcoming Emily in, and Jessie was standing there, ready to go.

"Come on in. Jake said you were coming by today. It's been a long time," said Betty pleasantly before asking, "Are you hungry?"

"No, I already ate, thank you. I thought I might steal

Jessie for the afternoon and go shopping if that's okay?" asked Emily.

"Of course it's okay, you girls have fun. Jake's busy anyway giving Mr. Thompson a hand with that tractor of his again. It seems he ran into his gate as he was mowing, or something like that."

Jessie laughed and said, "That's Mr. Thompson for you. He's does that just about every week."

"Is that right?" said Emily as the two left out the back door, adding, "We'll be back around six, Betty."

After sitting in the truck and buckling up, Jessie looked at Emily. "I want to thank you for last night, Ms. Jacobs. I don't know why I started crying; Grandma told me this was coming. I should have been prepared."

Emily looked over at Jessie with loving eyes and a soothing smile. "It's okay, sweetie, you're a young lady now. Please call me Emily. Can you do that for me? I would really like that."

Jessie nodded and, at that moment, knew the cordial relationship they shared across the diner counter had blossomed into something far more special and much stronger, a friendship that would last forever.

"So, are you ready to go do some shopping, Jessie?"

"I am ready… Emily."

They both started laughing as they set out for an afternoon of fun in Millsburg. Jessie liked going to the city, perhaps because it happened so seldom, usually once before school started and then again before Christmas. She enjoyed the beauty of the city snuggled at the southern end of Lake Tiohero in a narrow valley with the university perched high on the east hill. The city was captivating, with crowds of young college students mingling in cafes and shopping boutiques, along with the smell of freshly baked bread and pastries pouring into the Commons, a four-block pedestrian zone with cobblestone sidewalks, street lamps, benches, and trees.

Millsburg was much different from Cayuga Falls. There were young adults everywhere with tattoos, earrings, and hairstyles Jessie had never seen before, along with musicians and jugglers performing on the street as small crowds gathered to watch. The two of them spent the first hour or so strolling the Commons, browsing boutiques, sampling pastries, and relaxing to the street music before heading off to the mall.

Going shopping with Emily was a real treat for her. She provided a new and different perspective on fashion than either Betty or Uncle Jake offered. No more flannel and corduroy; today, they were shopping for high-rise jeans, cotton blouses, and appropriate undergarments a young lady would need. They spent hours moving from store to store, trying on this and that, until they found exactly what they were looking for. Emily paid for everything even though Jessie insisted that Uncle Jake would want her to pay her own way.

On the drive home, Jessie asked Emily, "Can we stop for a burger at The Pines? It will be my treat."

"Absolutely, sweetie, I worked up an appetite shopping. We can sit out on the terrace overlooking the lake; the weather is extremely pleasant."

The Pines was indeed a perfect place to relax and enjoy

the evening after shopping. As they sat there admiring the view, Jessie asked, "Do you like my Uncle Jake?"

Emily responded, "Of course, we've been friends as long as I can remember. We grew up and went to school together."

"I saw a picture of you two taken the night of the junior prom."

Emily smiled. "Oh yeah, I remember. Betty wouldn't let us out of the house until she had a picture of us all dressed up that night. I hope I looked good."

"Did you go to the senior prom?"

"No, as I recall, I was out of town that weekend visiting the University I was preparing to attend. I think Jake took Mary to the prom that year."

"Uncle Jake took my mom to the prom?"

Emily explained, "Of course she wasn't your mom yet. She didn't marry your dad for another year."

"So, Uncle Jake was dating my mom at that time?"

"I guess you could call it that. But it didn't last forever and eventually, your dad asked your mom to marry him just before he went into the Army. We were all kids back then, just growing up trying to figure out life and become comfortable with who we are."

Jessie paused and looked off in the distance. "And now, do you like my Uncle Jake, you know…?"

"Yes, I do. Just between us girls, I like him a lot, but he's a hard nut to crack, so it may take me a while."

"Don't tell him I told you, but he likes you also. Uncle Jake can't always find the right words to say how he feels."

After returning to the farm, Jessie thanked Emily again for a lovely afternoon of shopping. She felt very comfortable with their growing relationship and knew Emily would play a prominent role in her life going forward, and for that, she was extremely thankful.

Chapter 12

Under the Stars

July had passed, and the kids were in their final month of summer vacation. The boys spent much of their time playing basketball on the farm and going fishing whenever they could. Jessie helped make their transition from city life to Cayuga Falls bearable, and they would return the favor by inviting her and Shad over for a campout this weekend in their backyard. Mr. Jenkins spent Saturday afternoon helping the boys prepare the campsite, setting up the four-person tent, and making a fire pit while Mrs. Jenkins made snacks and cookies for the three of them.

Jessie spent the early morning hours at the diner with Jake and then mowed the yard before lunch. Afterward, she helped her uncle wash his truck and spent the rest of the afternoon riding her mini-bike around the farm. She was becoming quite the pro riding that little Yamaha, reaching speeds of nearly 40 mph, as she raced down the lane heading toward the lake, but her favorite part of the ride was zigzagging through the woods on the old snowmobile trail. The bike was very agile and nimble, and she felt confident in her riding abilities. She had even learned how to pull small wheelies and spin donuts but dared not to show off in front of her uncle.

Saturday evening found Jessie skipping over to the Jenkins place to meet up with the boys for their sleepover.

With her sleeping bag in hand and Shad beside her, they crossed Snyder Creek and made their way to the house. The front door swung open long before they reached the steps and Oscar came running out to meet them, hollering, "Jimmy's out back. Come on, we'll cut around the side of the house."

"All right," said Jessie. "Let's go, Shad, let's go find Jimmy," and off they went, racing around the house to the backyard.

Shad started barking, for he knew they were in for a grand time, and he wasn't about to miss out or be the last to reach the tent.

The sun hung just over the horizon, giving them approximately forty-five minutes to set up the inside of the tent with their sleeping bags, flashlights, comic books, and snacks before darkness set in. Outside the tent to the right was a lantern suspended from a low hanging tree branch to provide light after sunset. Mr. Jenkins was preparing to start the campfire now before it became too dark. The rest of the campsite saw four Adirondack chairs spaced around the fire pit with a blanket laid out on the grass next to the tent. Jimmy had whittled down three branches to use for roasting their marshmallows.

After starting the fire in the pit, Mr. Jenkins said, "You should be all set for the night. Make sure you douse the hot coals with the water from that pail before you go to sleep. The back door is unlocked in case anyone needs to use the bathroom. Have a good time; don't stay up all night."

"Thank you, Mr. Jenkins, the fire is very nice," said Jessie politely before the boys said the same.

"You're welcome," he replied, "Enjoy the smell of hickory."

As twilight turned to darkness, Oscar noticed a bright star just above the horizon and started chanting:

> *Star light, star bright,*
> *First star I see tonight,*
> *I wish I may, I wish I might,*
> *Have the wish I wish tonight.*

Jimmy said, "That's not a star; that's Venus, the second planet from the sun."

"Well, it looks like a star to me," replied Oscar, unfazed. "Can we start roasting the marshmallows while the fire is strong?"

"Sure thing," said Jimmy. "Let me get the bag, it's in the tent."

"Do you need any help there?" asked Jessie. "What can I do?"

"Yeah, you can grab those branches that I whittled down. They're right next to the tent."

"These little sticks look like spears; you did a nice job sharpening the ends. I'm sure they will work excellently," she said with a smile.

Oscar was the first to push a marshmallow on the end of his branch and stick it into the flames. After holding it there for ten seconds, the marshmallow caught fire, and Oscar was ecstatic. He whipped the branch back and forth through the air as if to perform some pagan ritual before blowing out the fire and swallowing the prize.

Jimmy was second to give it a try but left his marshmallow in the flames a bit too long, turning it black like coal before it melted and fell off into the fire. "Darn," he gasped as the other two laughed heartily.

Jessie smiled. "I don't like mine that black, I prefer them brown." She kept her branch a little higher near the top of the flame and rotated it slowly until it turned the perfect shade.

They spent the next thirty minutes sitting on the edge of their seats listening to the crackling of the fire, watching the ambers fly into the sky, and roasting marshmallows until the bag was empty, at which time there was still another log left to throw on the fire.

Oscar saw sparks flying in the distance and asked Jimmy, "How did the ambers get way over there?"

"What are you talking about?"

"Look, over there near the trees," said Oscar as he pointed toward the woods. "Don't you see those sparks? They're everywhere. What are they?"

"Those are fireflies," said Jessie. "Aren't they beautiful?"

"I've never seen them before," said Jimmy as he stared in awe.

"Me neither," added Oscar. "We didn't have those in the city. How do they light up like that?"

"I don't know how, but Uncle Jake says they light up to communicate with each other. We only see them in the summer, they're absolutely amazing."

"Dad was right when he said this was a great place to grow up as a child," replied Jimmy. "I can't think of a more peaceful and beautiful place than right here."

After throwing the last log on the fire, the three laid on

the blanket, looking up at the stars contemplating the universe. Jimmy had a detailed map of the constellations his dad obtained from the university science department. Using a small flashlight, he would choose a constellation on the map and then point it out in the heavens above. They could not have picked a better time of year for camping out or star gazing since the Perseid meteor shower was nearing its peak, providing an extraordinary celestial treat. Between the three of them, they counted twelve shooting stars, to which they each made a wish as it streaked across the sky.

Jessie closed her eyes tightly and thought, *I wish Uncle Jake would marry Emily.* She repeated that wish two more times to herself before opening her eyes.

"What did you wish for Jessie?" asked Oscar.

"I can't tell you, it's a secret."

By eleven o'clock, the meteor shower diminished, and the fire was out. Now seemed an appropriate time to throw the water on the hot coals and retire to the tent. As they laid in their sleeping bags, the conversation changed from scientific to philosophical, and within minutes, Oscar drifted off to sleep while the other two stayed up talking about the world.

Jimmy asked, "Have you been following any of the Olympics?"

"Do you mean the summer Olympics?"

"Yeah, I was wondering what you thought about the Soviet Union boycotting the Summer Olympics in Los Angeles?"

"I think it's stupid. These games are supposed to be about the athlete," said Jessie.

"My dad says it's all about politics. We boycotted their games in 1980, so now they feel they need to return the favor."

"I feel bad for the athletes that missed their chance to compete. I think it's totally unfair, but I think my uncle could really care less, one way or the other. Mr. Randall, my sixth-grade teacher, says the Olympic games help promote peace in the world. I think that is pretty important, don't you?"

"I agree. I think the games are important to everyone. I think most people, whether they live in the Soviet Union or the United States, believe in the same things. It's just our governments that are different. My dad always says history has a way of repeating itself, and he's a history professor."

"Do you know what I want to do when I grow up?" asked Jessie.

"What?"

"I want to be a pilot. Did you know women are now flying 747s? I would love to pilot one of those huge planes. Just think, you could be calling me Captain Jessica Peabody."

"You know, I can see that happening the way you fly around the farm on your motorcycle," he replied, laughing.

"No, seriously, maybe I will even become an astronaut after I learn to fly. My cousin Steven says the Soviet Union already has a female cosmonaut who walked in space. Grandma says I can do anything I put my mind to."

"My dad says the same thing, but I don't know what I want to do yet. I have some time to figure it out, though."

"Do you ever wonder about your parents – what they

were like before they got married, who they dated, or if they were even your real parents?

"No… Why?"

"I do all the time. Maybe it's because I never knew them. Do you think that's strange?"

"Not really. I'm sure it must be difficult. I would probably be curious, too."

They talked for another thirty minutes, mostly about the remaining two weeks of summer vacation and the coming school year, until neither could keep their eyes open any longer. Drifting off into never-never land under the stars with the sounds of cicadas vibrating, crickets chirping, and frogs croaking in the background was remarkably easy for three innocent children growing up in the lakes region.

Chapter 13

Unimaginable

It has been a great summer vacation so far. It's almost perfect, thought Jessie. *I have my own motorcycle, two new companions next door, and of course, my new friendship with Emily.* The only drawback was not spending as much time with her uncle as she did during the school year. She missed those rides into town every morning, walking to and from school and starting her day, as she would finish it, with her Uncle Jake. He was the rock in her world, providing stability, support, and strength, but in truth, he was much more; he was her world, and the bond between them was stronger than most.

Jake had assumed the fatherly role since Jessie's birth with a sense of responsibility owed to John and Mary. At first, he was unsure, even frightened about the prospect of raising her, but that all changed the first time he held her in his arms. Now, almost thirteen years later, and after two months of summer vacation, he understood what it meant, what it was all for, and with a sense of purpose and pride, he thought, "I am so lucky." He also realized just how grown up and independent Jessie had become, and like her, he missed those times they spent together every day.

The hot and dry weather pattern that persisted over the lakes region in June and July finally broke, and afternoon/evening thunderstorms became the norm, which was good news for the farmers. Last night's thunderstorm came with strong winds, along with thunder and lightning that shook the windowpanes in the old farmhouse. Jake and Jessie could still see the remnants and destruction left behind as they drove into town for their Saturday ritual. The ditches alongside the road were full of water and there was ponding in the fields along with a few trees down. As they turned south on Route 96, two sheriff vehicles traveling in the opposite direction passed them heading north. "There's our tax money, hard at work," commented Jake as they passed.

"When we get home, we better survey the farm and see if we have any trees of our own down. You definitely do not want to hit one of those riding that motorbike of yours," said Jake. "You could get hurt badly."

"Yeah, that sounds like a good idea," replied Jessie. "Running into a tree wouldn't be very good for sure," although she thought, *why would I run into a tree… I think I would stop before crashing into one.*

By this time, they had reached town and would park along West End Road, just around the corner from the diner. Jessie was excited about seeing Emily again, enjoying breakfast and seeing who was out and about this Saturday morning. As they turned off Main Street, looking for a parking spot, Jake noticed two more sheriff vehicles parked across the street. He thought, "How strange, I didn't even know we had that many deputies on duty… I wonder what they are all doing here in Cayuga Falls this morning."

"Okay, sweetie," he said while parking the truck, "Let's go see if they have any seats left at the counter."

The diner looked the same as usual: Emily was behind the counter, Richard was working the grill, and the air was filled with delicious aromas emanating from the kitchen. There were still plenty of seats to be had, including a few at the counter. Jessie and Jake took the last two at the far end of the counter next to the wall. It was still early, not quite seven, so it was sure to fill up within the next half hour.

Emily came right away with a cup of coffee for Jake and a small orange juice for Jessie and asked, "Do you need some time, or do you want the usual."

"I'm not sure yet," said Jessie. "I think I will take a look at the menu; I feel like something different today."

"Okay," replied Jake as he smiled at Emily. "I guess we'll be a few minutes. Looks like you've got some company today."

Emily glanced over at the deputies and then back at Jake, shook her head, and with a look of disbelief whispered, "It's not good." She then reached out and touched his hand, "I'll be back in a few minutes to take your orders."

Jake squinted in thought and wondered, *What's going on?*

Jessie hadn't taken notice. She was too busy looking at the menu and dreaming about what she would like for breakfast before deciding on Belgian waffles with strawberries and whipped cream and maybe some bacon on the side.

When Emily returned, Jake ordered first. "I'll have the usual over easy."

"How about you, kiddo," she asked with a smile, "what

would you like today?"

"I would like the Belgian waffles with strawberries and whipped cream. Can I get bacon with that?"

"Of course you can, sweetie. I will have them right out," said Emily.

Before handing Richard their order, she looked at Jake with troubling eyes as if to convey the sadness she felt inside. He could tell something wasn't right, but he wasn't sure exactly what it was.

The diner was not as loud as usual, and the conversations seemed much more muffled, as if everything was a big secret. Jake could feel something was up: four deputy sheriffs and their vehicles in this sleepy town on a Saturday morning, and Emily was not looking or acting herself. She obviously did not want to say anything in front of Jessie.

Breakfast took a bit longer to be served that morning, and Emily apologized for the delay as she slid their plates in front of each. "Sorry, Richard isn't quite himself this morning. Let me know if I can get you anything else."

"No, we're fine, thank you," said Jake.

Jessie didn't mind the waiting, especially after seeing the waffles piled high with strawberries and whipped cream; she was in seventh heaven. You would have thought she hadn't eaten in a week.

When they finished eating, Jake asked Jessie to go next door to the IGA and pick up a roast for their Sunday dinner. "Here's five dollars, let Linda know if that's not enough, I will stop by later to settle up."

"Is that all you want me to get?" she asked.

"That's all your grandma asked for, so that's what we'll

get. I'll finish my coffee and meet you at the truck, thanks!"

Emily was busy and didn't see Jessie leave the diner. When she looked around, Jake nodded and said, "We're ready when you are."

Emily asked where Jessie was and if everything was okay.

"We're good, thank you. Mom wanted me to pick up a roast for tomorrow, so I sent Jessie over to see Linda. Is everything okay with you? I can pick you up after work, and we can talk if you'd like."

"I would like that a lot," replied Emily. "I need someone to talk with today. I'm supposed to get off at noon, but it may take me ten or fifteen minutes more before I actually get out of here. I have to give Bobby the morning receipts and schedule."

"That's okay; I'll be waiting by the truck whenever you're ready."

Jake left the diner and walked around the corner straight to his truck. Jessie was already sitting inside, waiting with a grocery bag on the seat beside her.

"Do I owe Linda anything?" he asked.

"No, it came to four dollars and seventy-eight cents," replied Jessie. "Guess what? I know why there were so many cops in town this morning."

"Really, why is that?" he asked.

"Someone got shot last night."

"What," exclaimed Jake with a bewildered look. "How do you know that?"

"I heard them talking in the IGA. Linda said she could not believe something like that could happen here in

Cayuga Falls."

"Are you sure? Did they mention any names?"

"I heard them say Mark Hansen, but I don't know anyone named Hansen," she replied.

Jake knew the Hansen name well but did not let on. Instead, he changed the conversation back to the storm, knowing he would find out what happened later in the day when he saw Emily. "After you take that roast inside to your grandma, we'll drive down the lane and take a walk up the trail to see if any trees came down. I'll get the chainsaw."

Jessie grabbed the bag and ran inside. "Grandma, someone got shot last night, and we saw lots of cops this morning!"

"What on earth are you talking about, Pumpkin?"

"Well, I don't know what happened, but I heard Linda talking in the IGA about someone being shot. I think she said Mark Hansen, and then she said she couldn't believe that could happen here."

"That's awful," replied Betty with a puzzled look.

"I've got to go. Uncle Jake is waiting," she said as she ran out of the house with Shad leading the way.

Jake and Jessie spent the next couple of hours surveying the damage to the farm, which in the end seemed rather minuscule given the force of last night's storm. Apart from a few large branches ripped off here and there, Jake was pleased to find all shingles intact on the house and garage, and no trees were downed. Overall, the farm was in good shape, and the corn looked surprisingly good, considering how dry the first half of their summer was. Jake kept the conversation that morning focused on the storm, farm, and corn leaving their trip to the diner and news of a shooting behind. When they finished, he thanked her for helping and told her he was spending the afternoon with Emily and that brought a smile to Jessie's face.

Emily finished out her shift and found Jake leaning up against his truck as he waited for her. The two embraced, giving each other a friendly kiss. "Are you okay?" Jake asked.

"It's awful, Jake, absolutely unimaginable. Can we just take a walk," asked Emily.

"What happened? Jessie said someone was shot."

"It's worse than that, Jake. Marcus Hansen shot and killed his parents late last night. He then shot himself. How do these things happen?" She started crying.

Jake wrapped his arms around Emily and held her tight. "I don't know," he said softly. "I didn't know Marcus was even out or back in town, for that matter. The last I heard, he was still at Lake Ridge under evaluation. He had many problems. You know that, right?"

"I heard he was in rehab for drug use, but how can someone shoot their parents and then themselves? I just don't understand."

"Neither do I. What I do know is that damn war is still taking its toll, and Marcus is as much a casualty as anyone else. His natural father, Charles Hansen, was killed in Vietnam just months before John died. I think Marcus was about five at that time. Can you even imagine the impact? Hell, I was nineteen when John was killed, and it still haunts me. Anyway, his mother then remarried not long afterward and became a Stewart… What was his first name?"

"Michael, I think?"

"Yeah, that's right… Michael Stewart," replied Jake. "What a winner he was. Marcus got a raw deal the day Michael Stewart and Donna Hansen married. Michael was not a kind man; he drank a lot and had a violent temper. I can only imagine the abuse Marcus suffered. I think it screwed him up for life. The last I heard, he dropped out of high school and turned to drugs, and that's why they sent him to Lake Ridge Psychiatric Center."

"If he was that unstable, why did they let him out, Jake?"

"I can't answer that question, Emily. I'm guessing there will be a big investigation to find out, though. How did Richard take the news? He was friends with both John and Charles before they were both killed in action. Just thinking about the two of them tears me apart inside. It doesn't take a lot to bring those nightmares back to life. I think we were all victims of that war."

"I'm so sorry, Jake," she said. "I never considered how this would make you feel, or Richard for that matter. He was visibly shaken today at work, and I had no idea."

"It's okay. I've kept this inside for years, not wanting to acknowledge or talk about it, yet today, for some strange reason, I feel comfortable discussing it with you. It's hard to put into words."

They embraced each other again, this time holding each other tight for several minutes before Jake asked. "What am I going to tell Jessie? I know she's going to ask me. I hate for her to hear of such things… she's so young."

"Jake, you need to be honest and upfront with her, tell

her the truth. She's more grown-up than you think, and it will be far better coming from you than hearing it secondhand from some stranger."

"I suppose you're right," he said. "She told me that she didn't know any Hansen, but if I remember correctly, there was a girl with the last name Stewart who graduated sixth grade with her this year. Did Marcus have a half-sister?"

"I'm pretty sure I heard one of the deputies saying a younger sister was the only survivor. Apparently, she ran to the neighbor's house for help, and that is where they found her. Would you like me to be there with you when you tell her what happened?"

"I would appreciate that very much," replied Jake as they drove off. "You know she adores you."

Chapter 14

Reaction

Jake and Emily took the long way home giving them a chance to gather their thoughts. They drove south out of town on Route 96 before turning left on East Arden Road and passing the old Hansen farm where the mayhem that rocked the community took place the night before, leaving three people dead and one orphaned. The farm itself, except for two acres the house sat on, was sold off after Charley Hansen died. Many in the community felt Michael Stewart had only married Donna Hansen for her money.

They drove slowly as they passed the farm, trying to get a sense of what had happened. The house was in bad repair, with shingles missing, shutters broken, eaves troughs barely hanging on, and it probably hadn't seen a new coat of paint in twenty-five years. An old pickup truck on jacks sat in the driveway, missing its right rear wheel and tire. The yard was overgrown, with an old washing machine rusting away and junk scattered everywhere. It was hard to imagine anyone even living there.

Emily looked at Jake with misty eyes, "What's going to happen to the young girl that survived? Does she have any family here that you know of?"

"I honestly don't know," answered Jake. "I'm pretty sure she was Jessie's age. She will probably end up living with a relative, an aunt, uncle, or grandparents."

They continued driving east until they reached Lake Tiohero. From there, they turned north on Lake, a narrow, winding macadam road skirting the western shore. Neither Jake nor Emily said much as they drove along the waterfront; instead, they took in the natural beauty and captured the peace and solitude that Tiohero offered. The gentle waves caressing the shoreline as mallard ducks bobbed up and down were both mesmerizing and cleansing to one's soul. A great place to clear one's mind and gain perspective on life.

At nearly three o'clock, they drove down the lane to the farmhouse. There was no sign of Shad running from the house to meet them as usual, meaning Jessie was probably out and about with the boys next door. That would give Jake and Emily a chance to talk with Betty alone without curious ears eavesdropping. Betty met them at the back door, anxious to learn the news.

"Come on in," she politely said to Emily. "Would you like some coffee?"

"That would be nice," said Emily as she looked at Jake.

"I'll have some too, Mom. Where's Jessie, over with the boys?"

"Yeah, she'll be back before dinner. She's helping the boys clean up from the storm yesterday. I guess they had a tree come down behind their house last night. So, tell me, what is this I hear about a shooting? Jessie said there were all kinds of cops in town this morning when you went to the diner."

"That's right; I guess it was quite a chaotic scene last night. Marcus Hansen was let out of Lake Ridge Psychiatric

Center on a pass and shot both of his parents before shooting himself. Well, that being his mother and stepfather, Donna and Michael Stewart. Did you know them?"

"Not really; I did see Donna in town at the IGA from time to time with her daughter… Oh my God, what about the girl?"

"I'm really not sure; I heard she ran to the neighbor's house for help and wasn't shot," said Emily. "At least, that is what I understood the deputy to say. Does Jessie know the Stewart girl?"

"I'm sure she does," replied Betty. "They went to elementary school together and just graduated sixth grade. Let me find that pamphlet. Where did I put that?"

While Betty was looking for the pamphlet, Jake asked Emily, "Would you like some apple pie? I'm going to have a piece."

"Thanks, you know, with everything happening, I didn't even have lunch," said Emily as she felt her stomach growling.

"Yeah, me neither," said Jake. "How about I make us a couple of grilled cheese sandwiches to go with that pie."

"Sounds good to me," she said smiling, and then thought, *I serve people all day long; it's nice to be on the receiving end.*

Betty returned to the kitchen, and Roy followed slowly behind her using his walker. He heard the whole story while resting in the sitting room next to the kitchen. He felt his presence as the patriarch might be warranted, given the nature of the conversation.

Betty had the elementary school graduation pamphlet she was looking for in hand, and after placing her reading glasses carefully on her face, she scanned the sheet looking for the Stewart name. Finding the name took only a few seconds as they were listed in alphabetical order. There it was, Elizabeth Danielle Stewart.

"Donna did have a daughter," she said. "I knew it, her name was Elizabeth. If I'm not mistaken, I heard Donna call her Beth. Poor child… my heart goes out to her. I will pray for her in church tomorrow."

"I'll go with you Betty," said Emily, as she looked at Jake and gave a slight tilt of her head as if to say you should go also.

Jake grimaced and shook his head, saying, "I don't think so."

"Come on, Jake, I think you should go and take Jessie with you," said Emily. "It's the right thing to do."

Roy, who was standing with his walker next to Jake, looked him in the eyes and nodded in agreement as he mumbled, "We all go."

"Betty looked at Jake and said, "It's settled; we'll all go to church tomorrow… together and listen to what Pastor Paul has to say. This is what makes a community strong."

Jake was thinking, *Where the hell was the church and community for Marcus when Charley died? Where were they when he needed protection from an abusive stepfather? Where were they when he dropped out of school and turned to drugs?* Jake had a lot of unanswered questions, just as he did when John died, and he didn't believe the church held the answers to any of them.

Dinnertime was approaching, and Jessie and Shad finally found their way home. She was quite surprised to see the four of them in the kitchen together, especially Grandpa, who is usually found in the sitting room most of the day. "Did you find out what happened?" she asked excitedly.

"We did," said Betty, "but first, go wash up and then come and join us."

Upon returning, she said, "Well, what happened?"

Jake began, "Do you know Beth Stewart?"

Jessie's heart began to race with anxiety. She had not expected to hear that name, and her thoughts immediately flashed back to fourth grade before saying, "Yes, why?"

"She had a half-brother named Marcus Hansen from her mom's earlier marriage."

"Marcus Hansen?" said Jessie.

"Marcus was the son of Charley Hansen, who was killed in Vietnam. She never talked to you about her brother?"

"No, I didn't even know she had one." Her heart started to sink with expectations of what might follow.

"Marcus was a very troubled boy after losing his father," explained Jake. "His stepdad, Michael Stewart, was a violent man. He drank a lot and was very abusive, especially toward Marcus." Jake paused, looked down, and turned away trying not to show the memories and thoughts racing through his mind. "I'm sure the rest of the family also suffered from this abuse." He cleared his throat.

Jessie didn't say a word. She listened carefully, trying to process every word coming out of Jake, but she feared what had not been said.

"Anyway, Marcus was always in and out of trouble most of his childhood before dropping out of school and turning to drugs. He was eventually committed to Lake Ridge Psychiatric Center for evaluation. This weekend, he was given a pass to spend with the family, and for whatever reason, he shot and killed both Donna and Michael Stewart, Beth's parents, before turning the gun on himself and committing suicide. We will probably never know what made him pull the trigger."

"What about Beth, Uncle Jake?"

"She wasn't shot," replied Jake, "But I have no idea where she is or who she is staying with at this time. I can only assume she is with a relative."

Beth's survival offered Jessie a sense of respite after fearing the worst. But that feeling of relief was short-lived and soon gave way to anguish for her onetime friend's loss of family, particularly her mother. She couldn't imagine how Beth could even cope with such a situation.

Jessie knew all about growing up without her real parents, but somehow, it seemed different, much different. She never knew either of them and never had a chance to make a real emotional connection with them. Instead, it was her Uncle Jake and her grandmother who filled the void and provided love and security, the emotional connection a parent offers from day one. She never once felt the loss of a parent emotionally as Beth would, and that made her feel both lucky and sad at the same time. It would take a while to process what happened and to sort out her feelings.

As Jessie sat there deep in thought, Emily could feel the pain and emotions swirling inside her, "Are you okay, sweetie?"

"Yeah… I feel sad for Beth, losing her mom. I know it will be tough for her… I hope she will be okay," said Jessie woefully.

Emily knew exactly how Jessie felt and what she was thinking as she remembered the pain of losing her own mother, who died battling cancer. She felt and understood that same emptiness in her life, something no child should have to endure.

"We hope she will be okay, too, Pumpkin," said Betty. "I'll be praying for her."

Roy then muttered, "We'll go to church."

"Yes, tomorrow we will all go to church," repeated Betty.

Emily stood up and gave Jessie a comforting hug, "I better get going."

Jake jumped to his feet, "Okay, I'll drive you back into town so you can get your truck. It's been a long day."

As they left out the back door, Emily said, "I'll see you all tomorrow at church. Everyone have a good night."

Jessie spent the rest of the evening in her room thinking about Beth's situation and comparing it to her own, although they were in no way alike. At some point, she reached into her nightstand, took out the small box containing the picture of her mother, and read the wedding announcement cut out from the newspaper. After reading that announcement, she skimmed the article pertaining to her dad's enlistment. She then reread the wedding announcement. *That's strange,* she thought. He left for Ft Polk the day after the wedding. She was then struck with the realization that her birthday came only seven and a half months later. She didn't know what to think, but she was old enough to understand the implications.

Sunday morning came early, with the smell of breakfast filling the Peabody house. They needed to eat, clean up the kitchen, dress in their Sunday best, and be ready to leave by nine-thirty. This would be the first time they all went to church as a family since before Jessie was born, and that gave Betty a warm feeling, although she regretted the circumstances. Jake would drive Betty's car with her riding shotgun and Jessie and Roy in the back.

They arrived at the Methodist church in town across from the elementary school fifteen minutes before the service started. This gave them ample time to gossip with everyone before sitting and listening to Pastor Paul. After getting out of the car, Jessie looked across the street remembering the graduation ceremony that took place there nine weeks earlier. That was the last time she saw Beth Stewart and her heart sank thinking of her. She still regretted the rift between her and Beth and never forgave herself for being the cause. *Now, in light of what's transpired in the last forty-eight hours, she thought it seemed rather trivial.*

Pastor Paul came out, greeting everyone and inviting them in for service. He was surprised by the size of the crowd that came out to listen on this Sunday morning and waited patiently until all were seated and a hush fell over the church.

He spoke of the tragedy that beset the community before citing Psalm 34:18 and Mathew 5:4, *"The Lord is near to the brokenhearted; he saves those crushed in spirit. Blessed are those who mourn, for they will be comforted.*" He urged his congregation, "Hold on to your faith and stay strong for God, family, and community. Isaiah 26:3-4 tells us, *The Lord gives perfect peace to those whose faith is firm. So always trust the Lord because he is forever our mighty rock.* We are continually tested throughout our lives, not by the power of the Lord, but by man's own weaknesses, and we should never give in. Isaiah 30:18 says, *The Lord still waits for you to come to him so he can show his love and compassion. For the Lord is a faithful God. Blessed are those who wait for him to help them.*"

Before concluding the service, Pastor Paul led the congregation in a hymn, singing *Man of Sorrow* and ending with a short prayer. He then thanked everyone for attending service before inviting them all back the following weekend.

Emily followed Jessie out of the church, asking her what she thought of Pastor Paul's service.

"It was nice. I don't go to church regularly, so I can't say how it compares with other sermons, but it felt comforting."

"I like going," said Emily. "I see your grandma here every Sunday, along with most everyone else in attendance today. Coming here gives me a sense of community, friendship, and warmth. I wish your Uncle Jake would come with me."

"Maybe you should ask him," said Jessie with a clever smile.

"Maybe you are right, sweetie. I just might do that."

Betty, Jake, and Roy were last to leave the church, opting to wait until everyone else had cleared the aisle. This was the first time both Jake and Roy had attended church service since his stroke thirteen years ago, so they proceeded slowly as he maneuvered his walker one step at a time.

Emily gave Betty a hug and said she needed to get back to the farm and start dinner for her dad. Betty understood completely, as she needed to do the same thing for her family.

Before leaving, Emily gave Jessie a big squeeze and said, "If you need to talk, I'm right here, any time, okay Sweetie? Take care, I'll see you later."

She then turned toward Jake, taking his hands in hers, and with a firm grasp, said, "I'm glad you came to church with us today. I'm proud of you. Make sure you give Jessie a big hug and kiss tonight. She needs that reassurance. I'll see you tomorrow."

On the way home, Jessie thanked her uncle for taking her to church, saying how nice it was for them to be there together as a family. She thought, "We take too many things for granted, like family and friends, and vowed never to let anything come between them." The misfortunes that robbed Beth of her parents and siblings would strengthen her own relationships with everyone inside the Peabody household. She didn't understand exactly why or how, but she felt refreshed with a new perspective on life and family.

Chapter 15

Together Again

As promised, Emily dropped by the Feed & Seed Monday afternoon to see Jake after finishing her shift at the diner. The town was still reeling from the events of the weekend, and Emily had stood behind the counter all morning listening to it over and over with each new customer who came in and sat down. She was ready for a break, and she needed a warm hug and an ear to bend, which only Jake could provide.

Bob greeted her from behind the counter as she entered, "How was your morning? Are you busy over there?"

"Not really; everyone is still wound up from this weekend," she said. "I'm just tired of hearing about it. You know…"

"Yeah, I get it. How's Richard doing this morning?"

"He seems to be in a better mood today, at least more focused; he even tried cracking a joke this morning. What's Jake up to?"

"He's out back on the forklift unloading some seed that came in. Give him about ten minutes to wrap it up, and then he'll be free for lunch."

"Sounds good. I'll just wait out front in one of those nice-looking Adirondack chairs you have. They look pretty comfortable."

"Once you sit down in it, you won't want to get up,"

laughed Bob. "I can give you a special price on one."

Emily smiled and snickered, "We'll see."

Jake finished stacking the pallets neatly in the warehouse and joined Emily out front, offering a friendly embrace and a kiss on the cheek. "You look nice today. How was your morning?"

"It was okay. It could have been better if I didn't have to wait until noon to see you," she said warmly. "Anyway, I came over to talk with you about Jessie. She's been asking a lot of questions about you, me, John, and Mary and our relationships back in the day – who was dating who, and when, etc. I think she's searching for some answers, Jake.

"What kind of answers is she looking for? We've told her everything."

"Have you, Jake… are you sure?

Jake felt lost and hesitated in answering. "I guess I will talk with Mom and see if she knows what's going on. I appreciate you telling me."

"Of course, I just want the best for Jessie. She's becoming quite the young lady, and she's very intuitive. You need to be open with her."

The past began swirling around in the back of Jake's head. He felt his relationship with Emily growing stronger and cherished the idea of the two of them together, but he worried that Jessie's curiosity might impact the bond he had with her, and that scared him.

Emily knew that Jake was particularly guarded with his emotions but felt the time was right for the two of them. She also knew Jessie would play a pivotal role in their relationship.

What seemed like minutes in thought was actually only seconds before Jake asked, "Would you like to go to the movies on Friday night in Millsburg? Just you and me."

"Of course, that would be nice," she replied with a twinkle in her eyes.

"How about I pick you up at five-thirty, and we'll do dinner first?"

"That sounds even better," she said. "Are we going somewhere nice or fancy? Should I wear a dress?"

"If you want, I was thinking we could have dinner at the Old Victorian Inn at the Waterfront Marina. Everyone says it's nice inside and has great food. We can watch the sunset over the lake and enjoy the evening before taking in a late movie."

"That sounds perfect, I can hardly wait. I've been hoping to go there and check it out for quite some time. I've just been waiting for someone to ask me… Jake," she said with a bit of sarcasm.

Jake knew exactly what she meant and took comfort in her patience and persistence. They would see each other off and on throughout the week, either at the store or at the diner, both waiting in anticipation for Friday evening to come.

Monday evening at the dinner table, Jake told Jessie he was taking Emily out for dinner and a movie Friday night, hoping she wouldn't mind. Although the circumstances were far different, he remembered Betty scolding him for wanting to take Emily to the carnival, so he wanted to make sure there were no hard feelings.

Jessie was delighted hearing the news and said, "That's

great, Uncle Jake. I like her a lot, and she's very nice. I'm sure you both will have a good time."

Jake was relieved and said, "Thanks, I'm sure we will."

Thursday morning came, and Emily showed up at the Peabody house unannounced at ten o'clock. Jake was at work, and Betty was sitting at the kitchen table talking with Jessie, so Shad was obligated to greet her at the back door.

Emily knelt, gave Shad a big hug, and then said, "I hope I'm not intruding."

"Not at all," said Betty. "Come on in; what are you up to today?"

"Well, I thought I might borrow Jessie for a few hours. I need a new dress for Friday night. Jake's taking me out, and I thought she might be able to help me find something special."

"Can I, Grandma? Can I go shopping with Emily?"

"I don't see why not. That sounds like fun, Pumpkin."

"You're welcome to come along also, Betty, if you like," said Emily. "We can all go together."

"No, that's okay; I have things to do, but thank you for the offer," she replied. Betty knew that Emily was sincere in her offer but would rather see the two younger ladies spend time together. She could see their budding relationship blossoming and realized that Jessie needed a younger woman, someone Emily's age, to look up to and be a role model, and she could think of no one better suited than Emily for that role. If only Jake would open his eyes and heart and see what's right in front of him.

As they left the farm, Jessie said, "I'm glad you and Uncle Jake are going out Friday."

"Me too," replied Emily adamantly as she looked over at Jessie, "It's about time; after all, we are married."

"What?" exclaimed Jessie, "You're married?"

Emily laughed and said, "Not really, well, sort of."

Jessie was confused, and it was written all over her face. "I don't get it. How can that be?"

"It's a long story going back to third grade. You see, one day at recess, we were outside playing on the same playground that you played on right behind the elementary school. Anyway, you know those tall pine trees at the far end of the field?"

"Yeah," said Jessie.

"Well, it was right there on the last day of third grade that your Uncle Jake proposed and asked me to marry him."

"Really! I can't believe it," said Jessie as she began to laugh.

"Neither could I, but I said yes."

"Then what happened?" asked Jessie, begging for more.

"Well, we needed a preacher, someone to perform the wedding ceremony. The closest person to us was Donnie Brewer, so Jake went over and asked him if he would do it. The rest is history. After saying a few brief words, Donnie pronounced us man and wife, you can now kiss the bride."

Jessie was laughing so hard she had tears in her eyes. "My Uncle Jake got married. Wow, I can't believe it."

"I still remember that day clearly, but I think we should keep this just between you and me, sweetie. I don't know how Jake feels about that marriage."

They spent the rest of the afternoon at the Commons, visiting several boutiques until she found the perfect dress, an elegant, soft, floral print with pleats and a front tie. With a rounded neckline and short sleeves, the dress fell just below the knees, showing off her calves and flattering her figure. "This was the one," she thought, and Jessie agreed.

On the way home, Emily looked at Jessie and asked, "How are you doing? I know you've had quite a summer and seen a lot of changes. How do you feel about everything that's happened?

"Mostly, I feel okay," she said, looking down but sounding a bit melancholy. "I do feel sad at times… for Beth and her situation. I think maybe we are both victims of the war, just in different ways. You know, sometimes I think I know nothing about my mother, and it's a little confusing. Uncle Jake and Grandma talk very little about her or my dad, and there's hardly any pictures."

"Well, sweetie, you know your mom and I were best friends growing up. She and John were an awful lot alike; he was the captain of the basketball team, and she was a cheerleader. She was also the prettiest girl in school and had all the boys wrapped around her little finger. I still miss her."

Jessie wanted desperately to ask Emily a question, but was uncertain of what she might think or say. Instead, she took a moment to reflect on the void in her life before turning and looking her straight in the eyes. Then, with a little more enthusiasm, she added, "It has been nice, though, having the boys move in next door. We've had an exceptional time together this summer. Mr. and Mrs. Jenkins are really nice, and I do feel lucky, very lucky, to have Uncle Jake, my grandparents and you. I hope we can be friends forever."

Jessie's words touched her heart deeply. She reached over, taking Jessie's hand in hers, and with a firm grip, answered, "We will always be the best of friends, sweetie, I promise you, forever."

Jake asked Bob if he could leave work an hour early on Friday evening telling him about his big date with Emily and how they would spend the evening in Millsburg going to dinner and taking in a movie. Bob was fine with him leaving early and was glad to finally see Jake moving on. He always thought those two would make a fine couple and wished him the best. Jake hurried home right at four o'clock to shower, dress, and look his best before picking up his date.

As he pulled up to the Jacobs' house, he was as giddy as a sixteen-year-old on his first date. Before reaching the porch, Emily appeared in her new dress, high-heeled sandals, and purse. "Simply stunning," he said. "Wow, you look… amazing!"

"Thank you," she replied, "You don't look too bad yourself."

He reached out, taking her by the arm, and escorted her to his truck. He opened the door in a gentlemanly manner and said, "Are you ready for a good time?"

"I am," she smiled, and off they went.

The Old Victorian Inn was everything it was said to be – charming, elegant, and sophisticated. Built in the late 1890s, the house was originally constructed for the founder of Millsburg Rifle Company, which employed only the best blacksmiths and machinists in the early twentieth century.

It was painstakingly renovated in the early Seventies and turned into a restaurant/inn, where its proximity to the waterfront and marina made it very romantic.

Jake knew this night would be a defining moment in their relationship. He also knew Emily was ready to make that commitment and that it was time for him to stop hiding and surrender to his emotions. They had been friends forever, but the attraction and the emotional bond were far greater now, and he could feel her warmth capture his heart. He was in love with Emily, and he had been for a long time.

Jake started to speak as Emily said, "I need to say something."

"Okay, you go first," said Jake.

"No, that's okay, you go first."

"Okay. Do you remember the first time we kissed under the pine trees in third grade? I will never forget that day; I've had a crush on you ever since, and now I find myself drawn to you more with each passing day. I know I'm not the easiest person, and I tend to hide my feelings, but I can't hide them anymore. I don't want to hide them anymore."

Emily reached across the table with caressing hands and warmly said, "You don't have to hide your feelings from me, Jake. I'm here for you; I will always be here."

After dinner, they strolled along the waterfront holding hands, enjoying the lights shimmering on the water while listening to the smallest of waves splash against the boats anchored in the marina. They stopped for ice cream and laughed as they recalled their first wedding under the pines some twenty years earlier. They were lost in time but rejoiced in the knowledge that they found each other once again.

Jake had not felt this alive in thirteen years, and as he gazed into the starry night, he knew an angel had unlocked the chains that bound his heart. Emily felt blessed as well and thought *this was truly a wonderful evening.*

The sun was already up when Jake came sneaking into the house. He had just dropped off Emily for her Saturday morning shift at the diner and wanted to change into something a little more casual before heading back for breakfast. Betty sat at the kitchen table and said with a big smile. "Looks like someone had a good time last night."

"I did, thank you. Is Jessie up yet?" he asked.

"I don't believe so. You better go change before she sees you."

Jake showered quickly and changed into a pair of faded, worn jeans and a T-shirt before yelling upstairs to Jessie, "You better get up if you want to go with me this morning."

"I'll be right down," she said. Seconds later, she and Shad raced through the kitchen and out the back door.

On the drive into town, Jessie said with a smirk, "Looks like you had a good time last night."

"I did. Why do you say that?"

"I noticed the hood on your truck was still warm," she said, giggling.

Jake looked at Jessie and grinned. "I don't know what you are talking about."

"You don't have to pretend, Uncle Jake. I think it's nice that you and Emily are together."

Chapter 16

One on One

The last week of August was upon them, and summer vacation was nearing its end. With only ten days left before the official start of school, teachers, administrators, and staff were all back in their jobs, gearing up for the new year, working on bus schedules, class assignments, syllabuses, and so on. The tempo in Cayuga Falls was picking up after a lazy summer, and this meant more business at the diner on weekdays. Emily did not mind, though; she knew everyone in the community and enjoyed the interaction. Bob and Jake were just as busy at the Feed & Seed this time of year, delivering winter wheat seed orders to farmers in preparation for their fall planting season that was only a few weeks away.

In the meantime, Jessie was enjoying what little time she had left on break before conceding to a new school regiment. This meant planning a few more trips to the lake with the boys to test out their luck at fishing, hiking through the woods along Snyder Creek, riding her motorbike, and playing basketball in the barn. Of course, Shad would be there every step of the way with her and the boys as he was part of the team. However, she soon found out that the best-laid plans do not always come to fruition, as Mother Nature had her own ideas.

The weather pattern over the lakes region changed, and

September rains came early, bringing cooler temperatures, overcast skies, and a never-ending drizzle, forcing Jessie and the boys to squash some of their plans. The basketball court in the barn was renamed the Peabody Dome and would become their home for the next few days until the weather broke. Basketball was still high on their list of things they like to do, especially after watching the U.S. Men's Olympic team win gold at the Summer Games. They spent hours trying to emulate their favorite star's abilities, showing off their moves and throwing up prayers, which would find the bottom of the net every now and then.

Jimmy thought a competition should be held at the Peabody Dome, their own summer Olympics to speak of, and he outlined plans for the games, saying, "Tomorrow, we will play for gold; I will represent the United States; Jessie, you can be Spain; and Oscar, you will be Yugoslavia." Those three teams just happened to be the ones who won the gold, silver, and bronze medals, respectively, at this year's Summer Olympics.

Oscar asked, "Why do you get to be the United States?"

"Because I'm the oldest, and I will probably win," he said confidently.

"That's fine with me," said Jessie, who had plans of her own for an upset. "It's okay, Oscar. Just because they won gold in July does not mean they will win tomorrow."

"Do you want to make a bet on that?" asked Jimmy with an air of conceit.

"I'm not betting on anything," answered Jessie resentfully, "I'm going to show you."

And so, the competition was set. They spent the rest of

the afternoon practicing and scouting each other's moves, and by the end of the day, each was confident in their abilities and thought they would emerge victorious in tomorrow's game. The competition would be one-on-one, with the first person scoring ten baskets declared the winner. In the first round, each person would play two games. The two with the best record would then play for the gold. In the event that all three were tied after the first round, they would start over.

After a good night's sleep, a hearty breakfast, and an hour of warming up, the games began precisely at ten o'clock. Jessie won the first game 10-6 against Oscar, earning her a break while Oscar and Jimmy squared off. Oscar was no match for Jimmie either, losing 10-4 in a rather physical match. With two losses, Oscar was out, but Jessie and Jimmy would still play their first-round game to see who would have the better record going into the final match. This game proved to be much more competitive than the first two matches, with Jessie prevailing 10-8 after a hard-fought battle.

"Take that," said Jessie with an air of confidence. "You didn't think I had a chance, did you?"

"I let you win that one," replied Jimmy with a smirk. "You won't be so lucky in the next game."

Oscar, who looked up to Jimmy, said, "You're going to lose the next one, Jessie; he's better than you. Besides, you're a girl."

This infuriated Jessie and only proved to increase her determination to win. *I'll show them,* she thought.

The final game for the gold went back and forth,

changing leads half a dozen times. With the game tied at nine, each missed several attempts to win before Jessie finally banked a fifteen-foot jump shot from right of the free throw line.

Jessie jumped in exhilaration, pointed her finger at Jimmy, and said, "Take that! A girl just beat you for the gold."

Out of frustration, Jimmy grabbed the basketball and with a swift kick, punted it like a football as hard as he could. The ball soared high across the court, ricocheting off the roof before landing in the loft high above.

"Don't be a sore loser," Jessie said. "I beat you fair and square." She then scurried up the ladder to fetch it while the boys took a breather. The ball found its way to the far corner of the loft, coming to rest behind some boxes, and it took a few minutes to locate. After retrieving it, she walked toward the edge of the loft, yelling down at the boys, "Do you think I can make it from up here?"

"No," they both exclaimed at the same time.

After giving it considerable thought and calculating exactly how much arc to put on the ball, she gave it her best shot. They all watched in anticipation as the ball made its way toward the rim. It was as if everything was in slow motion and then *swish*... nothing but net. Jessie was screaming with delight, and the boys were left in awe.

How could that be? Jimmy and Oscar thought.

"Are you ready to lose another game?" she asked before climbing down from the loft. "I'm just getting warmed up."

Jimmy was about to surrender when he heard a sharp crack come from the direction of the loft. In her excitement to get back on the court, Jessie missed the second rung of the ladder, and when the full weight of her body hit the third rug with gravitational force, it gave way, splitting in two and sending her crashing to the floor with a loud *thud*.

Jimmy and Oscar rushed to her side in disbelief as she screamed out in pain, crying for her Uncle Jake. The pain was overwhelming, and all three were in tears.

"Go get Betty, hurry Oscar!" shouted Jimmy. "Run!"

Oscar ran as fast as he could back to the farmhouse with Shad leading the way, barking up a storm.

Jessie was crying uncontrollably, screeching in pain, calling out for her uncle.

Oscar burst through the back door of the house crying while trying to tell Betty that Jessie had fallen and was badly hurt. "You've got to come… hurry, please!"

Betty jumped to her feet and tried to stay up with Oscar as they ran toward the barn. She could hear Jessie shrieking in pain before they were halfway there, and she didn't know what to think. As they entered the barn, she could see Jessie lying on her back, crying out with her leg twisted to the side. "Oh my God… Jimmy, go inside and call 911. Hurry; tell them exactly what happened and that we need an ambulance immediately. The phone is hanging on the kitchen wall; hurry!"

Jimmy raced to the house following Betty's orders. He had never called 911 before and wasn't sure what to expect.

"911, is this an emergency?" asked a voice at the other end.

"Yes, we need an ambulance; hurry, she's hurt badly," said Jimmy.

"Okay, I understand, sir, stay calm. What is your name?"

"Jimmy Jenkins."

"Thank you, Jimmy. What is your address?"

"We're at the Peabody farm on Old Hills Road, three miles east of Route 96 outside of Cayuga Falls."

"Thank you. What is the nature of the injury?"

"A broken leg for sure, I'm not sure what else. She took a bad fall, and she's in a lot of pain."

"Okay, Jimmy, we have an ambulance on the way. What is the name of the injured person?

"Jessie Peabody," said Jimmy.

"Thank you. Please stay on the line."

Roy heard the commotion in the kitchen and made his way there slowly with his walker. He understood from the conversation that Jessie was hurt badly. Roy muttered, "Thank you," and made his way out the back door. His trip to the barn would take several minutes using the walker.

Betty and Oscar were in the barn at Jessie's side, trying to comfort her as much as possible, given the situation. Betty asked Oscar to go into the house and fetch a blanket to keep her warm. As he raced toward the house, he passed Roy, pointing back at the barn, and said, "They are inside."

Both Jimmy and Oscar returned to the barn a few minutes later with a blanket for Jessie and news that an ambulance was on its way. Another fifteen minutes would pass before the ambulance arrived.

Betty tucked the blanket around Jessie, making sure not to touch or move her leg for fear she might make the situation worse. She held Jessie's hand tightly telling her everything would be fine and that paramedics were on their way. "Just hang on, Pumpkin," she said. "Be strong, it will be okay."

Jessie continued to sob, although her shrieking subsided to a steady moan and complaints of pain. She was conscious and understanding that her leg was broken, but her whole body hurt from the fall. It had all happened so fast, coming as a complete shock. It took a while for her to regain her senses. "It hurts Grandma; it hurts terribly… I'm sorry. I didn't mean for this to happen."

"Shhh… I know, Pumpkin."

Soon, they heard the sirens off in the distance. Betty asked Jimmy to run to the road as quickly as possible and flag down the ambulance telling them they were in the barn. "Hang on, Pumpkin," she said, "they are almost here."

Thank God for 911 and paramedics, thought Betty. She was amazed at their knowledge, their professionalism, their understanding of the situation, and how quickly they were able to address her condition and ready her for transportation, all the while making her feel as comfortable as possible. Betty would ride in the back of the ambulance on the way to the hospital with Jessie, but before leaving, she gave Jimmy instructions to call Jake at work. If he could not reach him there, he was to try Emily at the diner. She then hugged both boys, assuring them that everything would be okay and thanking them both for helping Jessie through this emergency. She also asked them both to make sure Roy made it back to the house safely.

Chapter 17

The Patient

Jimmy and Oscar walked Roy back to the house and explained everything that happened in detail. Once inside, Jimmy asked Roy if he knew the telephone number for Agway so he could call Jake and tell him what happened. Roy pointed to the telephone book containing the Yellow Pages sitting at the end of the counter nearest the phone and motioned for Jimmy to bring it to him while muttering the same.

Jimmy dialed the number twice, but no one picked up the phone at the other end. "No one is answering," he said, looking at Roy.

Roy nodded his head. "Emily."

"Right," answered Jimmy, but first, he would need to find the telephone number for the diner. The number for Agway was easy to find as it started with "A" and was circled with a black magic marker. "What's the name of the diner, Roy?"

"Emily," he said.

Jimmy shook his head in disbelief but turned to the pages, and there, under "E," was a listing for Emily's Diner. He dialed the number, and after the third ring, a voice at the other end said, "Emily's, can I help you?"

"Is this Emily?" asked Jimmy.

"Yes, it is; how may I help you?"

"This is Jimmy, Jessie's friend. She's had a terrible accident, and they are taking her to the hospital."

"What kind of accident… and who's taking her to the hospital?" Emily asked anxiously, knowing that Jake was at work. Jimmy began giving Emily the whole rundown when she stopped him and said, "Thank you, I have to go."

She hung up the phone and turned toward Richard, "I have to go; I have an emergency. Bobby will be here in a few minutes to take over." Bobby was Emily's youngest brother and co-owner of Emily's Diner.

"Of course," answered Richard, "I've got it, no worries."

Emily split out of the diner and raced across the street to find Jake. "Where is he?" she asked while trying to catch her breath.

"Jake is on a delivery right now," replied Bob. "Why?"

"Jessie fell from the loft in the barn and broke her leg, she's hurt pretty badly. She's being transported to the Medical Center in Millsburg by ambulance right now. I've got to let him know."

"Give me a minute to lock up, we'll take my truck." He ran to the back, pulled down the overhead door, and returned in a hurry, saying, "Let's go." As they climbed into the truck, he proceeded to tell Emily that Jake was out at the Powell farm making a delivery. They would meet him there, and she and Jake could take his truck to the hospital, and he would finish the delivery.

"Thank you, Bob, I can't thank you enough," she said with a worried look on her face.

When they reached the Powell farm, Jake was standing

alongside Mr. Powell with a clipboard in hand going over the invoice. Both looked up at the truck that was kicking up dust as it came barreling toward them. Jake recognized the truck right away and wondered, *What the hell?*

Bob came to a screeching halt, as Emily flung open the door and sprung from her seat. "Jake, you have to come – it's Jessie. She's hurt badly."

"What?" exclaimed Jake.

"I'll tell you in the truck, let's go."

Jake ran to the truck, and they both tore out there, tires spinning and gravel flying. "Where am I going?" he asked, looking over at Emily.

"Upstate Regional Medical Center."

"What happened? Is she okay?" he asked nervously.

"I don't know… I only know that she fell from the loft and broke her leg and was hurt badly, Jake. Jimmy Jenkins called me at work and said she fell while they were playing basketball in the barn."

Emily slid over to be next to Jake. In turn, he gave her a quick kiss and rested his hand on her thigh as they made their way to the hospital. They remained quiet the rest of the trip, both deep in thought, worrying about Jessie and wondering just how bad her injuries were.

After reaching the medical center, they sprinted across the parking lot and ran into the emergency room, asking the receptionist about Jessica Peabody's whereabouts. Seconds later, before the receptionist had time to answer, Betty was by their side giving Jake a hug saying, "Come over, we can sit over here and wait, it's going to be a while."

"How is she, Mom? Is she going to be okay?"

"I think so, but she's hurt awfully bad, Jake; she has a broken leg for sure, possible ruptured spleen, a few cuts, and lots of bruises. She's in a lot of pain."

"Can we see her?" he asked, fighting back the tears.

"Not yet; they took her down to radiology to get pictures of the leg and abdomen," said Betty. "They did give her something for pain when she first came in."

Emily tightened her grasp on Jake's arm to comfort him and said, "She'll be okay, Jake, she's in good hands here. Let's go get a cup of coffee."

"We'll be back in a few minutes, Mom; do you want us to bring you anything?"

"No, I'm okay," she said nervously, "I already had a cup. It's just down the hall on the right."

They returned shortly and sat next to Betty, waiting for news. Twenty minutes turned into forty minutes, which turned into an hour before hearing anything. Finally, Dr. Schmitt, the attending emergency room doctor, approached them with an update on Jessie's condition. After introducing himself, he pulled up a chair, and they all sat down, listening intently to every word he spoke.

"I won't sugarcoat it. She's hurt badly, and it's going to take some time for her injuries to heal. She has a displaced, comminuted fracture of the left tibia. That is this bone right here," he said, pointing down to his lower left leg. "It is going to require surgery, and that could take a couple of hours. Dr. Coats, an orthopedic surgeon, is on his way and should be here soon. She is still in radiology and is currently undergoing a CT scan of her abdominal area, primarily the left side. I'm concerned about her spleen. She was complaining about pains in the upper left abdominal area, and she has some external bruising there. X-rays came back negative for broken ribs. The scan will give us a better picture of what's happening on the inside. The pain medicine I gave her on arrival seems to be working. We'll try to keep her as comfortable as possible while we assess and treat her injuries. Do you have any questions for me?"

"How long before we will be able to see her?" asked Jake.

"I cannot give you an exact time, but it is going to be quite some time from now. We still need to look at the scan and see what's going on inside with the spleen. I expect that she will be in surgery for one or two hours for the fractured tibia, followed by an hour or so in the recovery room. If the spleen is just bruised and not ruptured, you might be able to see her in about two and a half, maybe three hours, but that will all depend on how the procedure goes. If we have to go in and remove the spleen, it will be even longer. Now would be a good time to take a break and maybe get something to eat. You might want to consider making plans to stay here for the night, but that's up to you."

"Thank you," said Emily as Jake and Betty were still processing the information.

"Are you okay, Jake?" asked Emily.

"I'm okay, I'm just thinking…" said Jake. "I think we better go home, give Bob his truck back and Mom needs to make Dad some dinner. Shad is probably hungry, too. I'll take a quick shower, put on some clean clothes, and come back for the night.

"I'll come with you, Jake," said Emily warmly as she

reached out for his hand. "I won't be able to sleep anyway; I would rather be here for you and Jessie."

"Are you ready to go, Mom?" asked Jake.

"I guess. I hate leaving my Pumpkin here alone."

"She's not alone, Mom; she's well cared for and has the best doctors. You need to be home for Dad. He's probably going out of his mind wondering what's happening. I should have called him, I didn't think…"

The sun was still high in the sky at four o'clock when they returned to Cayuga Falls and gave Bob his truck back. From there, they piled into Jake's truck and headed off to the farm, but first, he would swing by the Jacobs place and drop off Emily.

"I'll see you in about an hour," he said, "Will that give you enough time?"

"That will be fine," she said, giving him a kiss. "See you soon."

Jake and Emily returned to the hospital just before six in the evening. They asked the Emergency Room receptionist if she could give Dr. Schmitt a message telling him they were back and if they could get an update on Jessica Peabody. It took only ten minutes for Dr. Schmitt to find them and provide an update.

"I have some good news for you; her spleen is not ruptured, just bruised. Dr. Coats has finished surgery and should be out here in a few minutes to give you an update on her leg. She's resting comfortably right now in the recovery room. I think it will be another 30 to 45 minutes before she's moved into her room for the night. I will let you know as soon as that happens so you can see her."

"Thank you, Doctor; I appreciate everything you've done," said Jake with a sense of relief. "I can't wait to see her."

"It won't be long," replied Dr. Schmitt. "Here comes Dr. Coats now; I'm sure he can give you a better update on her leg than I can."

"The surgery went well," said Dr. Coats, "The tibia was fractured in two places. We had to insert a couple of plates and several screws to put it back together. It does look good, however; there was very little in the way of tissue damage, and it happened just below the growth area, and that is a good thing. We will keep her in the hospital for the next couple of days, monitoring her bruised spleen and ensuring she doesn't develop any infection. It's going to take a little time, but I expect she will recover one hundred percent. She's in the recovery room now, and they are getting her room ready. You should be able to see her within the next half hour."

Emily and Jake were overjoyed with the good news and called home to let everyone know. Betty and Roy would sleep better knowing their little pumpkin would be okay, Bobby was thrilled to know he had to open the diner in the morning, and Shad, well, he wouldn't understand where everyone was and would be restless most of the night.

A nurse finally came and escorted Emily and Jake to Jessie's room, where she laid in bed with a plaster cast on her left leg, half-conscious and still groggy from the anesthesia. They stood there by her side, holding her hand and smiling.

"Hey, Sweetie, how are you doing," asked Emily, "Can

you hear me?"

"Yeah," she answered softly.

"You gave us quite a scare," said Emily gently.

"I'm sorry, I didn't mean to."

"You don't have to be sorry," said Jake as tears rolled down his cheeks, "accidents happen. We're just thankful you will be fine. It's going to take some time, though, but we will all be here for you. We love you more than you will ever know. Try to get some rest."

Chapter 18

Past, Present, and Future

Seeing Jessie laying there in the hospital brought back painful memories for Jake, memories so painful he just wanted to forget or pretend they never happened, memories that stole from him everything he loved, tearing a hole in his heart he thought would never heal, memories you try to escape from but just can't, ask Marcus Hansen or his brother John Peabody and they would tell you if they could, "there is no escape." It's been said that "time heals all wounds," but for some, they last a lifetime, tucked away in the far reaches of our cerebral cortex, waiting for someone or something to pull that trigger, waiting to explode and tear out your heart once again.

Twelve and a half years ago, Mary was admitted to this same hospital. To Jake, it felt like only yesterday. As he sat there watching over Jessie, his thoughts flashed back to that day and the conversation they had. Mary was extremely weak and in pain and about to give birth to a baby girl that would be named Jessica Peabody. Jake was barely twenty.

"Jake," she pleaded, "promise me you will take care of Jessica. She will need someone strong and sensitive like you to be in her life."

"You will be able to take care of her yourself," he replied. "She's going to need her mother more than me."

"Just promise me, Jake, if something happens to me, you

will be there for her. I need to know that you will care for her and love her like your own."

"Of course I will, Mary; John was my brother."

"She's of your blood, Jake."

"I know. I'm her uncle, and I will take care of her and help you as much as possible. I promise you."

"I'm so sorry I hurt you, Jake. I had no idea John was going to ask me to marry him, and I certainly didn't know I was pregnant at the time. I don't even know why I said yes when he asked, I just felt compelled for some reason. Maybe it was the fear of uncertainty in his eyes, knowing he would be sent to Vietnam. I don't know. When I think back, I'm not even sure John would have asked me to marry him had he not been drafted into the Army. Before that, he was the most outgoing person I knew; he was the life of the party, and everyone loved him for that, including me. I could only hope that I would live up to his expectations and that he would love me forever. We got married the following week, a day before he left for boot camp. I didn't discover I was pregnant for another two weeks, and then he was sent to Vietnam. Things never got better after that day; they just spiraled out of control, and the letters he sent home sounded so distant and depressing. I never expected that he would be killed in action. I'm sorry about everything, Jake, and I hate myself for what I did. If I could take it back and change things, I would, but I can't."

"You're not the only one who feels bad, Mary. I thought you felt something for me. Was that just a lie? I loved you. What will people say?"

"You have nothing to be ashamed of, Jake. You did

nothing wrong. I should have never, never said yes. I thought if I married John, you would be able to marry Emily; you two were meant for each other. No one will ever know except for you, Jake. Everyone will believe she is John's daughter and your niece. You have to promise me you will take care of Jessica forever. She's yours, Jake."

"I don't know…"

"Jake, listen. I'm trying to tell you… John and I were never intimate before he was deployed to Vietnam. He was too distracted, too preoccupied, what with the war and all. I've tried to tell you a dozen times, but I just couldn't find the words. I never told John I was pregnant and hid my pregnancy as long as I could. When I finally told your mom, she naturally assumed it was John's. After he was killed in action, I couldn't bring myself to tell you the truth, but I have no choice now. I'm sorry for what I did, and the Lord will judge me, but I'm not sorry for having Jessica; she is going to be a shining star in your life."

Jake didn't know what to say or what to think. He just sat there staring into space.

Mary gave birth to Jessica Peabody later that afternoon by cesarean section. She lost a considerable amount of blood during the procedure and spent the next two days in intensive care before passing away. She never had the opportunity to hold Jessie in her arms. The coroner determined the cause of death to be a blood clot.

Jake was devastated – he lost his brother John two months earlier and now Mary. His world was slowly falling apart…

"Jake, Jake… wake up. Are you okay?" asked Emily,

shaking his arm and trying to wake him.

"What... Oh… I must have dozed off, what time is it?" said Jake, as he yawned.

"It's nearly five in the morning. You two slept most of the night."

"I don't know how; this chair isn't that comfortable. Did you get any sleep?"

"A little, but I woke every time I heard her moan, poor thing."

"This place haunts me; it's like a nightmare. The last time I was here, Mary was lying in that bed."

Emily whispered to Jake, "Shhh…" and mouthed the words "she's awake."

Jake rubbed his eyes, pushed himself out of the chair, and stood beside the bed looking down at Jessie. "How do you feel, Sweetie?"

"Sore… my left side hurts right here," she said as she rubbed her lower left rib cage with her right hand, "And my leg is throbbing a little bit," she said with a grimace. "But it doesn't hurt as much as it did yesterday."

"The nurse came in about midnight and gave you some pain medicine," said Emily. "Do you remember her coming into the room last night? You were moaning quite a bit but slept much better after that."

"No, I don't remember her. I do remember having a dream last night, and Uncle Jake, you were in it. It all seemed so real."

"I hope it was a nice dream and not a nightmare," said Jake with a smile.

"I dreamt that you were my dad, and I saw my mother

too. We were all on the farm together, walking down the lane toward the lake. It was strange, though; you were holding my hand, and we were trying to stay next to her, but we couldn't. She was running too fast, chasing a dove that was flying toward the lake. I wanted to reach out and tell her that I love her, but she just vanished in a heavenly light."

Emily and Jake looked at each other, raised their eyebrows, and shrugged their shoulders before Jake said, "It was probably John in your dreams with Mary."

"No, it was definitely you in my dream, and you were my dad, I swear," said Jessie.

"Dreams can be insightful and confusing at the same time, sweetie," said Emily. "They often tell us about our emotions. It's only natural after a traumatic injury that you might have a dream about your parents. After all, they are supposed to protect, nurture, and comfort you. I can't think of anything more traumatic than your accident yesterday. I cannot even begin to imagine how scared you must have been."

"That was the most scared I've ever been," she replied, "and the pain was unbearable. I thought I was going to die. I just wanted Uncle Jake to come and make everything okay."

Emily smiled and, with a comforting touch said, "God was watching…"

Before she could finish, the door opened, and a nurse, along with the attending doctor, entered and greeted them with a "Good morning. How are we doing today?"

"Fine," said Jessie before realizing that she really

wasn't. "Well, actually, my leg is throbbing a little, and I'm still sore. Oh, and I'm also hungry."

"I'm sure we can find you some breakfast. Let me take a look," he said, sliding the blanket over, revealing her left side and cast. He placed his hands on her abdomen in several places, applying palpation to check for tenderness while visually checking the bruising. He finished with a check of her toes to make sure her circulation was fine and that the cast was not too tight. "Well, kiddo, everything is looking good this morning. We're going to give you something to help with the pain, but you're still going to feel some soreness for the next few days." He turned to Jake and Emily. "She looks good; we are going to keep her one more day just to watch her labs and to keep weight off that leg. I don't foresee any issues at this time. Dr. Coats will be in later this morning."

Emily, Jake, and Jessie all thanked the doctor and nurse for their time before they left to continue their rounds.

Jake turned to Emily. "Speaking of hungry, I am too. How about you? Do you want to get some breakfast?"

"I am a little hungry," replied Emily.

"Okay, well, I think we are going to go home for a little bit, sweetie, to shower, eat and change clothes. We'll be back later this morning. Are you going to be okay with that?" asked Jake.

"I'm okay," answered Jessie. "Can you bring me my book when you come back? I'm reading *Call of the Wild.* It's on my nightstand."

"Can we bring you anything else?" asked Emily.

"No, not that I can think of. I will be okay, thank you. I

do want to thank you both for being here and staying with me all night."

Emily bent over the bed and brushed her fingers through Jessie's hair, giving her a warm kiss on the forehead. "Any time, sweetie, I will always be here for you. I'll see you later. How about we bring you your toothbrush, PJs, and hairbrush with that book when we come back."

At the same time that Jake and Emily left the hospital to return home, Susan, Jimmy, and Oscar were leaving their house to come visit Jessie. It would be a welcomed surprise and brighten up her morning. They came bearing gifts, some flowers, a book on *Modern Aircraft,* seeing Jessie wanted to be a pilot when she grew up, and some colored magic markers for all to sign their names on her cast. She enjoyed the attention she was receiving, but more than anything else, she cherished the love and friendship of those who meant most to her.

Chapter 19

More to Say

Before going home, Jake and Emily swung by the diner in Cayuga Falls to have some breakfast, see her brother, and pick up the truck that she left there yesterday. She also wanted to thank Bobby for taking her shift and to let him know she would be back at work once Jessie was home from the hospital and that she appreciated all his support. Running the diner can be challenging when only one of them is there.

Bobby said, "I don't mind," and then joked, "You're paying me double for these days anyway."

Emily smiled, "Don't worry; I'll take care of my favorite brother. Seriously, I really do appreciate it, thanks!"

The three of them engaged in small talk while they waited for Richard to finish making breakfast. Several faculty members and administrators from the elementary school were also enjoying breakfast at the diner prior to hashing out the final details of next week's school opening. Jake recognized many of them, including Mr. Atkinson and Mr. Randall, who came over and said they heard about Jessie's accident, asked if there was anything they could do, and wished her a speedy recovery. Jake thanked them both and said he would pass on their kind words to Jessie, who should be coming home tomorrow.

When they finished breakfast, Jake and Emily went their

separate ways. Jake drove straight home to the farm while Emily took the long way home, first swinging by the bank to drop off the diner's deposits. They made plans to return to Jessie's bedside and visiting with her that afternoon. After a quick freshening up, Jake would drop by the Jacobs place at noon to pick her up.

Before going into the house, Jake walked out to the barn to get a feel for what happened. "How exactly did Jessie fall from the loft and break her leg?" That was the question he kept asking himself. It didn't take him long to find the broken rung on the ladder and understand what happened. He pictured her crashing to the floor, sending shivers up his spine, and with a sense of guilt, looked down, closed his eyes, and rubbed his forehead, wondering. *Am I responsible? Could I have prevented this accident?* These questions remained unanswered but would torment him for the next few days.

In the meantime, Shad was patiently waiting at the back door for Jake to come in from the barn; Betty was in the kitchen, and Roy was in his chair. All three were glad to see him, especially Betty.

"How's my little pumpkin doing this morning, Jake?" she asked impatiently. "When is she coming home?"

"She's fine, Mom. The doctor said they are keeping her one more day just to be on the safe side, although he said she's doing well. Emily and I are going back this afternoon to see her again and stay through the evening, but we'll come home tonight after visiting hours. Did you want to go with us?"

"I would love to see her, but I think it best if I stay here and get things ready for tomorrow when she comes home. That extra bedroom downstairs needs straightening up, and I need to put some clean linen on the bed. I fear she won't be able to climb up and down those stairs for quite some time with that cast on her leg."

"It's a good thing we've got you around, Mom. I would have never thought about it."

"I also need to bring her bath necessities downstairs. Roy and her can share the shower and bathroom down here for the next couple of months."

"Anything else?" asked Jake.

"Yes, I want to decorate the house and celebrate her homecoming, you know, to cheer her up a little bit. I will bake her favorite chocolate cake this afternoon and invite Susan, Gene, and the boys over tomorrow for a little celebration, maybe around eleven or noon. What do you think?"

"I think that sounds like a swell idea; she will appreciate that for sure. Is there anything that Emily or I can do to help you?"

"No, I think I can manage okay," she said. "You just bring that little tyke home tomorrow with you."

Time passed quickly before Emily and Jake made it back to Jessie's room, where they found her sleeping peacefully. Susan, Jimmy, and Oscar stayed until noon and left when lunch was served.

Emily drew the curtains closed, making the room a little darker. "She's so sweet, Jake. Look at her, you're such a lucky man."

"I know, she's a keeper; she's the best thing that ever

happened to me. I cannot tell you how much I love her."

"And me, Jake, what about me?" teased Emily.

"And you, let me think," said Jake playfully with a grin, "Oh yeah, I have a special place in my heart for you also," and after a slight chuckle, added, "Seriously, I love you both, and I am extremely lucky to have two such beautiful ladies in my life."

Emily embraced Jake with a soft, slow kiss. "I will never come between you two; I love you both too much for that, and I love having you both in my life." After a long embrace, they sat quietly, waiting for Jessie to wake up, thinking about their lives, their future, and what comes next.

Another hour passed before Jessie woke and asked, "How long have you both been here and what time is it?

"It's close to four," said Jake, "You must have been tired."

"I was. I think lying in this bed makes me tired. Oh, you know what? Jimmy and Oscar visited this morning after you left. Mrs. Jenkins is so nice; she brought me those beautiful flowers over there on the table and the boys got me this book on the history of modern airplanes."

Emily went to the window and opened the curtains to let in the afternoon light. "How's that leg of yours feeling, sweetie?"

"Better, but it still hurts a little. I can feel a slight throbbing pain from my foot to my knee. Dr. Coats said it would be sore for the next week, but the pain should gradually subside. Look!" she said, sliding the blanket to the side, revealing her cast. She already had five get-well messages written in various colors on her cast.

"Wow, now that is what I call art," said Emily with a smile.

"Yeah, it is nice; everyone who comes in the room signs it with a little message. You both need to write something."

"I know exactly what I'm going to write," said Emily, as she took the blue marker and began: *Wishing on every star that you get better soon! With love, Always, Emily,* adding a few small stars for effect. "Your turn, Jake."

Writing cute little messages was not something that came easily for Jake, but he remembered what Mary said to him, and he wrote: *You are my shining star, get well! With love, Jake* with a small little heart at each end.

Jessie was very pleased with what they wrote, especially with the word love, which she knew to be true and that meant everything to her. They spent the next few hours enjoying each other's company, discussing *The Call of the Wild,* and looking at pictures of modern planes. Jake and Emily both had something to eat from the hospital cafeteria and pretended it was delicious. They spoke with the doctor and nurse who dropped in on their evening rounds. Everything looked good for Jessie being discharged in the morning. Eight o'clock came before they knew it, and visiting hours were over. After many hugs and kisses and saying goodnight, Emily and Jake would take leave and head home.

As they got closer to Cayuga Falls, Jake decided to turn right onto East Arden Road, heading toward the lake before turning north on Lake Road.

"Where are we going," asked Emily as she sat close to

Jake.

"I thought we would drive along the lake and check out the light. It's a beautiful night, and we don't have to get up early tomorrow."

"Sounds romantic," she said, leaning in a little closer.

Jake didn't say much as he drove along the lakeshore; his mind was too occupied with what he was about to say when they reached their destination. After ten minutes or so, Jake pulled off the road into a small parking area nestled between the lake and the road. Emily knew this place well and had fond memories of her and Jake coming here as kids, fishing, swimming, and even stealing a kiss or two.

Jake helped Emily out of the truck, grabbed a blanket, and said, "I thought we could sit here for a bit, look at the lights on the far side of the lake, and listen to the waves break against the wall like we did when we were kids."

"I would like that," she said as they walked down the steps hand in hand before sitting and dangling their feet above the water. Emily sensed that Jake had something pressing on his mind that he needed to say and gave him time to gather his thoughts.

"Jessie adores you, Emily. I know that I'm her uncle, but I think of myself as more. We are like family."

"You are Jake, you are much more than her uncle; you're her father."

"In a sense, yes, I know, but that was thrust upon me because of the circumstances."

"Jake, I'm trying to tell you Mary was my best friend, and we had no secrets. I know everything, and I know she wished that she never married John."

"What else do you know?" asked Jake inquisitively.

Emily looked at Jake with knowing eyes, "I know that acorns do not fall from pine trees."

"What?" said Jake with a confused look, "Can you repeat that?"

"I said that Jessie is not John's daughter; she's yours. I've known that since the day Mary discovered she was pregnant. She told me."

Jake was overwhelmed; he couldn't believe what he was hearing. He held this secret for thirteen years, not knowing that anyone else knew or even suspected what transpired, and tonight, he finds out that Emily knew the truth all along and never said a word. It took a few minutes for him to process and understand what he had just heard before saying, "I had no idea you knew; I've kept this secret inside of me since the day Mary died. Please don't say anything to Jessie. I don't want her to think differently of John or Mary." Jake hesitates. "Damn, does anyone else know?"

"I don't think so."

"I hope not, I wish to keep her world intact. What she doesn't know won't hurt her."

"Jake, you should know that I've kept this secret inside of me all these years, just as you have done, but I think it's time for the truth to come out. I would never do anything that would hurt either you or Jessie; you both mean the world to me, you know that. Listen, we cannot have any secrets between us… between you, me, or Jessie."

"You're right," he said, feeling the weight of the world being lifted from his shoulders.

They embraced for several minutes, holding each other

tight, before Emily said, "I have this feeling you still have something more to say."

"I do; I'm just searching for the right words… I wanted to know if you could accept Jessie as your own; she really adores you."

"Why Jake," she said, "If I didn't know any better, I would swear you just proposed to me for a second time."

Jake looked at her nervously and said, "I suppose I did."

"Well, my answer is still the same. The same as it was on the last day of third grade when you asked me to marry you under the pines. You know, this time, you will need to ask my dad for his permission," said Emily with a serious tone and a bit of a smirk.

"Of course, we will do it right," said Jake sincerely. "First thing tomorrow morning, right before we go pick up Jessie at the hospital, I will ask your dad for your hand in marriage along with his blessing. Then later, we can make an announcement to everyone at the party after we get back from the hospital."

"First, we should tell Jessie in person before we announce it to the world, Jake. I know she will be happy, but she needs to hear it from us; we can tell her together."

"I agree. I think we should tell her when we get back to the farm. It will be a comfortable setting to break the news."

They sat there late into the night, snuggled together in the blanket underneath the stars, listening to the waves break against the shoreline and dreaming of a new future together. As they held each other closely, Emily pointed to the sky. "Look… do you see those three bright stars near the Milky Way? Together, they form the Summer Triangle, a constellation with a story of love that was meant to be. That's us, Jake… you, me, and Jessie."

Chapter 20

Chasing Doves

Jake woke early the following morning, going straight to the garage for his tools and some wood necessary to mend the broken ladder that still troubled him. He was determined to fix it before Jessie or the boys set foot in the barn again. As he cut and nailed the boards in place, he realized it wasn't the ladder that was bothering him after all but rather the idea of letting the truth come out after all these years. After taking out his frustration in the barn, he returned to the house for his morning coffee.

Betty was already up making breakfast for the three of them, told him to have a seat, and asked what he was doing out in the garage so early in the morning.

Jake knew his day of atonement had arrived. "Mostly thinking about the past, Mom. I haven't been completely honest with you, Dad or Jessie. I've made a complete mess of everything."

"What are you going on about, Jake?"

"While Mary was in the hospital, before giving birth to Jessie, she told me that I was the father. I didn't know what to do, so I said nothing. I let everyone believe John was the father." Jake put his head in his hands, looked down, and began to cry.

"Jake, it's okay, look at me. To be honest, I always suspected, but I held my tongue because of your dad's heart attack and stroke. I wasn't sure how he would cope with that news. I'm just as complicit in this charade as you are."

Jake tried wiping the tears from his face, but they continued to flow as he spoke. "Jessie's been asking a lot of questions about the past – about mine and John's relationship with Mary, about who was dating who, and when. I think she suspects, but I don't know why or how."

Betty turned around and pulled a small box down from the cupboard. "I found this in her nightstand drawer while I was moving her things."

"What?"

"She's curious, Jake, and she deserves to know the truth."

Jake collected himself. "How can I look her in the eyes and tell her that I've lied to her all those years? What will she think of me?"

"She will love you like she always has… like the father you've always been." Betty slid Jake's breakfast in front of him. "Eat up, you will feel better."

Jake wasn't sure about that. Acknowledging he was Jessie's father was a relief, but his guilt went much deeper. Thirteen years ago, in a fit of rage and jealousy, his last words to John were, "I never want to see you again." The enormity of those words weighed heavily upon his conscience. Words he regretted saying and wished he could take back a thousand times; words that will stay with him as long as he lives.

"Are you listening to me, Jake? You need to tell her soon; she needs to know. Don't worry about your dad. I will tell him."

"I know, I will… but there's more. I also said things to John that morning he left for the Army, things I'm not proud of, things I shouldn't have said and feel guilty for saying."

"We all say things in haste that we don't mean, Jake. If I had a dime for every time I said something I shouldn't have, I'd be a rich woman."

"I told him I never wanted to see him again, Mom, and then he died."

"Jake, your words didn't kill John. The war did. You need to forgive yourself. What's past is past." Betty wrapped her arms around Jake and kissed his head. "Come on, eat up. You will feel better." What she didn't tell Jake was that she had written a letter thirteen years ago to John congratulating him on becoming a father-to-be in which he wrote back explaining that he was not the father and that he was sorry. That letter was postmarked the day John died.

"I'm sorry, Mom, I've got to go. I need to pick up Emily. We don't know how long it will be before they release Jessie, but we figured we should be there by nine. I did see the cake you made, and it looks delicious. Thanks for making it and hanging those decorations. I know Jessie will love it."

"I don't mind," said Betty solemnly, "I can't wait to see my little Pumpkin. I've got the room downstairs all set up nice and special for her. I invited Susan and the boys over for a little celebration later this morning. She said Gene couldn't make it; classes at the university had already begun, and he was too busy."

Jake wanted badly to tell Betty that he proposed to

Emily last night and that she accepted but did not want to give away their big surprise. He wanted Emily to enjoy the moment and see the happiness in their eyes when they broke the news together. It wouldn't be long before the cat was out of the bag.

Jake gathered himself, climbed into his truck, drove down the lane, and turned right on Old Hills Road, making his way to the Jacobs farm. A drive that normally took him less than five minutes seemed like an eternity that day. His mouth was dry, his palms sweaty, and his heart racing as he walked to the front porch, where Emily met him with a smile and a kiss.

"Come on inside, Dad is in the kitchen. "I haven't told him anything… Are you okay?"

"Yeah, I'm okay."

Seth, hearing the front door shut as Jake and Emily walked in, turned and said, "Morning Jake, what are you up to today?"

"We're bringing Jessie home from the hospital this morning," replied Jake.

"Right, of course. I heard she took quite a fall in the barn; that's too bad," said Seth. "Emily, are you going to stand there or get Jake some coffee? Let's all sit down."

Emily rolled her eyes at Jake and thought, *Oh no, here comes the inquisition.* Knowing her dad well, she was sure they were in for a lecture of some kind.

"Yeah, it was a pretty nasty fall, Seth; she broke her left leg in two places. The good news is she's doing well, and the doctors expect her to make a complete recovery."

"That's nice," said Seth with a hint of compassion.

Emily looked at Jake and then her dad. "Jake has something he wants to say."

Jake gave Emily a questionable look with a slightly furrowed brow as if to say *really* before continuing. "Yeah, there is something I wanted to say. I asked Emily to marry me last night, Seth. We would like your blessing."

Seth laughed, "Is that right? I thought you two were already married… just kidding. It's about time, Jake. Hell, you kept her waiting long enough. If this is what you both want, then you have my blessing."

Emily got up from her chair, walked behind her dad, gave him a big kiss on the cheek, and said, "Thanks, Dad!"

Seth reached over the table, shook Jake's hand, and welcomed him to the family. "Okay, so when's the big wedding day?"

"We haven't decided on a date yet. We are going to discuss that later today. First, we need to be on our way so we can pick up Jessie."

As they left the farm, they were both relieved that step was over and even though they knew what the outcome would be, they were still thankful. Emily asked Jake if he had a chance to talk with Betty.

"I did."

"Well, what did she say?"

"She said I needed to tell Jessie the truth and soon."

"Your mom is a smart woman."

When they arrive at Jessie's room, they were surprised to find it empty. They looked at each other, wondering where could she be. A couple of minutes later, Jessie came hobbling into the room on crutches, saying, "Check it out," behind her, a physical therapy technician giving her instructions and some advice.

"She's doing well, don't you think? She's been practicing for the last fifteen minutes. I will let you be so you can get out of that hospital gown and into something more comfortable. Let me see if I can find the charge nurse and ask what needs to be done to get her discharged."

"Thank you," said Emily. "We brought some sweatpants to go over that cast of yours, sweetie, along with a sweatshirt. The weather is quite dreary today, overcast, wet, and breezy."

"You were looking pretty good on those crutches," said Jake. "How's that leg of yours this morning."

"A little sore, but not awfully bad. You two look nice today. I like your scarf, Emily; where did you buy it."

"Actually, your uncle Jake gave it to me as a birthday present a few years ago. I think this is the first time I wore it."

"I love the doves on it; it's pretty," said Jessie.

Emily looked at Jake with a smile and said, "I like it also."

"How's Grandma and Grandpa? Did they miss me?"

"Everyone's fine and anxious to see you," answered Jake as he grappled with a more serious question.

"I can't wait to be home. I miss Shad and sleeping in my own bed."

Another twenty minutes passed before all the necessary paperwork required for discharging a patient was completed, and an aide arrived with a wheelchair to escort Jessie out of the hospital. Jake left first to bring the truck around to the entrance since it was still raining.

While waiting, Jessie looked up at Emily. "Is Jake my father?"

Emily bit her lip and shook her head as if to say I can't tell you, but her eyes said it all. As she wiped away the tears, she knelt down, taking Jessie's hands softly into hers. "Only Jake can tell you that for sure, sweetie."

"That's okay, Emily. I've often wished it to be true."

After a warm embrace, Jake pulled up to the curb, jumped out, and opened the passenger side door. Jessie found it a little awkward climbing into the truck for the first time with her cast on, but it was easier than she imagined. Emily got in on the driver's side and sat in the middle, close to Jake.

"Well, are we all ready to go home?" asked Jake.

Emily looked at Jake with moist eyes. "I think Jessie wanted to ask you a question?"

"What's that?" asked Jake nervously.

Jessie looked at Emily, then at Jake. "Are you my real father?"

Jake began to tear up; he cleared his throat before wiping away the tears, but his words still came out raspy. "I am… and I can't tell you how sorry I am for never telling you. I wanted to, but…"

"I think I understand."

Jake could not believe something so profound could come from someone so young.

Jessie reached over, touched Jake affectionately, and looked at Emily. "Thank you for everything."

As they journeyed home from the hospital, Jessie

thought back on the summer months remembering all that transpired. She recalled Mr. Atkinson's kind words and Mr. Fleming's insight, Emily's compassion, and the boys' camaraderie. She appreciated her uncle's, or rather Jake's, fatherly presence and her grandparents' wisdom and realized how life can be both precious and fragile at the same time. She understood that you cannot always control or even foresee the worst life has in store, but took solace in knowing she was surrounded by a network of family and friends who loved, nurtured, and cared for her every single day. She realized that it's not the title that defines a person but rather their character. Her mind raced through those long summer days to the tempo of the wiper blades moving back and forth across the windshield as if they were turning the pages of her life. Before she knew it, they were pulling off the road and heading down the lane toward the farmhouse, where she spotted Shad running toward them.

"He knows you're coming home today," laughed Jake. "He really missed you."

Jake parked his truck in front of the garage and helped Emily out on his side before running around to open the passenger door for Jessie. "Okay, let's take it easy getting out," said Jake. "We don't want to go back to the hospital today."

Jessie slowly slid herself sideways, facing out of the truck. Jake took hold of her arm, steadying her while she carefully stood up, balancing herself against the door. Emily retrieved the crutches from the bed of the pickup and held them for Jessie, who said, "It sure is nice being home on the farm. Look at that; the clouds are parting, and the sun's coming out." She then pointed her head toward the lake. "Is that not a beautiful sight?"

They all stood there gazing over the lower fields and the lane that divided the farm in two as it made its way east and downward toward the lake. There, in the distance, a rainbow appeared out of nowhere; a brilliant spectrum of light and color stood as a gateway to the eastern reaches of the farm. Behind it, they could see Lake Tiohero, an amazingly blue sapphire nestled in the valley below, shimmering like a diamond.

Jake felt this was a good time to break the rest of the news to Jessie. After looking at Emily and smiling, he turned, facing Jessie, rubbed his chin with his right hand, and said, "I have something else I would like to… well, we would both like to share with you. Last night, I asked Emily to marry me."

Jessie was overjoyed, her heart full of warmth and tenderness. She had wished and prayed for this moment all summer, secretly longing for someone to fill that void in her life and that someone was Emily. Excited, breathless, and pleading for an answer she already knew but needed validating, she asked, "Well, what did you say… Did you say yes?"

"I told him my answer was the same as it was on the last day of third grade when he asked me to marry him under the pines."

Jessie could no longer control her emotions, for she knew the story well. She was laughing and crying at the same time as she said, "I can't believe it! The two of you are finally going to tie the knot and get married, congratulations!" She turned and gave Jake the biggest hug ever before turning to Emily to do likewise. As she looked into Emily's eyes, tears flowed down her cheeks, and with a child's love, she said, "I don't know why I'm crying; I am so happy."

Tears began rolling down Emily's face as well as she replied with a comforting touch and gentle kiss, "These are tears of happiness, sweetie. I love you." Emily took off her scarf and said, "I want you to have this." As she placed the scarf around Jessie, a gust of wind snatched it from her hand, and it flew eastward down the lane toward the lake. "Oh my gosh!" she exclaimed, tearing after it.

Jessie looked on in amazement; she couldn't believe what she was seeing right there in front of her. "Look… look there!" as she pointed toward Emily. "That was my dream. That is what I saw in my dream; she was chasing a dove flying toward the lake except… except it was my mother… wait…" and then she realized exactly what she saw and smiled.

Jake was speechless. He didn't know what to think as he stood there watching Jessie's dream come to life.

Emily finally caught up with the scarf and returned short of breath from somewhere under the rainbow. "Can you believe that? The wind snatched it right out of my hands. Heck, I thought it was going fly all the way to the lake. I wasn't even sure if I could catch up with it."

Both Jake and Jessie looked at each other in amazement but said nothing.

"What's wrong with you two? You look like you've seen a ghost," said Emily as she wrapped the scarf around

Jessie's neck.

The two of them smiled and started laughing before Jake said, "I think we should go inside. I'm sure Mom and Dad are eager to see us." Emily handed the crutches leaning against the truck to Jessie and helped her get them situated. "Shall we go, sweetie?"

"I'm ready," she said, and they all made their way to the house.

Jessie had no idea what was waiting on the other side of the door. Betty, Roy, and Susan were all sitting at the table while Jimmy and Oscar tried hiding behind the door. Decorations were hung from the kitchen cabinets, and a vase full of flowers adorned the table.

As she came through the door, Betty and Susan jumped to their feet, and everyone shouted, "Surprise, welcome home!"

Betty gave Jessie an enormous hug. "I've missed you so, Pumpkin. It's nice to have you home. I made you a chocolate cake."

Jessie could hardly contain her excitement. "Did you hear the news, Grandma?"

"What news is that?" asked Betty.

With a smile on her face, Jessie pointed at Jake. "You better tell them."

Betty looked at Jake with a smile of relief and anticipation, wondering what he was about to say. Emily looked at Jessie, who looked at Jake, who looked at everyone else, and with a huge grin on his face, said, "Emily and I are getting married."

The kitchen erupted in cheers and congratulations, with

hugs and kisses from everyone.

"That's wonderful," said Betty. "Let's all sit down and celebrate; I want to hear all about it. We've got cake, ice cream, coffee, and tea."

As they sat around the table enjoying the moment, Jessie thought back to her wishes made on a shooting star, the dream she had in the hospital, along with her prayers and believed in her heart that this was a miracle, a divine intervention. She looked at Emily and whispered in her ear, "Wishes, dreams, and prayers can come true."

Emily smiled and whispered back, "God works in mysterious ways."

The End

Characters

Jessie Peabody	Mr. Randall
Jake Peabody	Ms. Carter
Betty Peabody	Mr. Atkinson
Roy Peabody	Lori Palmer
John Peabody	Ronnie Richards
Mary Peabody	Linda Johnson
Seth Jacobs	Allan White
Emily Jacobs	Rich White
Bobby Jacobs	Diane White
Bob Fleming	Marge Jackson
Richard Fleming	Harriet Carter
Gene Jenkins	Pat McDonald
Susan Jenkins	Linda McDonald
Jimmy Jenkins	Steven McDonald
Brian Oscar Jenkins	Mr. Thompson
Donna Stewart	Pastor Paul
Michael Stewart	Donnie Brewer
Beth Stewart	Mr. Powell
Marcus Hansen	Dr. Schmitt
Charlie Hansen	Dr. Coats

www.ingramcontent.com/pod-product-compliance
Lightning Source LLC
Chambersburg PA
CBHW040826010826
48978CB00012BB/625